To my besties; Jacquie, J
and Brown Bear, for ev∈   ₋ you put
on a scary film after a night out and then fell asleep.

Dear Pippa,

Sweet dreams with
your bedtime reading

Katie
x

1

Chapter One

The Neighbours, the night of

A scream in the night began it.

Darkness is brief and can only cover the corners.

At two in the morning when man slumbers as a dog, and the night sits on you like a heavy sodden blanket, the brutal ice-pick screams of a child will be written off as the twisting rape of a cat, the screeching rubber of tyres, a horror film played too loudly in the apartment next door.

But only for so long.

A child may scream at night when caught up in the inevitability of her nightmares, or the taunts of her own burgeoning imagination; the thing under the bed, the man-beast shape that leers and creeps, dry lips cracking as a sickly smile works its way across the face of it, showing rotted teeth and libidinous intent.

But those screams calm and settle with the reassuring footsteps of parents, the turning on of a bedside light, the forever warmth of a mother's touch, the velvet armour of a father's words, *'there there little one, nothing's coming, daddy's here.'*

But when those screams continue, their vibrations beating like fervent wings, *you neighbours*, hiding under the false promises of sleep, wake you now to all the dreadful possibilities. Climb out of that dreamless river that hides you, open your eyes to a world where the persistent screams of a child are as impossible to ignore as a fire alarm.

2

Yes, we know, this isn't fair. It's cold outside and you've a video call with the CEO about a Congeneric Product Extension Merger at 7.00a.m.

Yes, we know, those screams are clearly coming from the apartment across the hall, and yes, *yes*, you'll reach her long before the emergency services do.

And yes.

As you cross bare footed towards them, and their sound is now more that of a dying animal, some piteous lamb being slowly devoured by a tiger, yes, we know, you're about to witness something that means life will never taste quite the same again.

"Martin! Martin! What's going on in there?"

"Open up!"

"Have we called the police?"

"Has anyone called the police?"

"Yes, yes."

"Yes."

"We did."

"Clark did."

"Jenny is at home, she' on the phone to them now."

Manic screams roaring from the other side of the Miller's apartment door silenced the accumulated neighbours' bickering and collectively reminded them why they had assembled there in the dead of night.

"We can't wait."

"Ok, come on, get the other big guys up here. Fast."

The Millers, the night of

The couple swayed together as in a dance. She seemed drunk at first, draped heavily over him, hair fallen over her face, arms lolling over his shoulders, feet being dragged as they gently slid this way and that across the tiles, rather than moving with any conscious intent of their own.

He, steady and unswerving, held his love so tight against his chest that when the burliest of their neighbours broke through the front door and followed the child's screams, which were now slowed to a desperate whimpered gasping, and found them in their unison, they seemed almost fused together by glue.

Outside it had begun to snow apple blossom petals, flakes of pale pink twirling as they cascaded through the moonlight.

Who knew a kitchen could be so romantic?

Just as the neighbours began turning to each other, wondering what all the screaming had been about, the man brought his arm back, bent at the elbow, and thrust it towards his love.

She jolted with the force of it, and the blood that pulsed out of her and dripped down her leg to join the growing pool beneath her gleamed in crimson-black. It was not the first of her wounds and would not be the last.

As if on cue, the child took to her screaming again. Not the first of her screams, not the last.

She had crammed herself so tightly between a cupboard and the freezer that none of the neighbours had spotted her at first.

It was only when the trembling warble-wine of her whimpers, rose to the mighty crescendo of murder-shock shrieks that they remembered in unison why they had battered down the door.

4

Women, and the elders of the neighbourhood collective, crowded round the shoulders of the men, gasping, crying, some joining the girl in her screams, many pushing, urging to get forward to reach her, the men's heavy arms holding them back.

The man thrust the knife once again into his partner's lifeless corpse as he continued his overkill.

The men nudged and tussled each other, about to stampede, bulls readying to be let out of a pen.

He stopped his onslaught, looked over to them, mildly surprised by their presence, then to the dead woman in his arms, even more surprised by hers.

He blinked savagely, trying to wake himself from the dream.

"Martin, my god, what have you done?"

Their eyes danced from him to the dead woman, to the eleven year old girl squashed like a bug against the white goods, the dolly in her hands the only one smiling as she gazed out with button blue eyes at the chaotic blood soaked scene.

"What have you done to your family?"

He turned to look down at the girl.

His eyes hit her, as sharp as the knife in his hand, she squirreled back, cramming herself even deeper into an impossibly small space, an octopus manipulating itself into a glass jar.

He turned back to his neighbours, as if for help, his beleaguered eyes begging them.

They could do no more than shake their heads, no answers to be pulled from such a night gone mad.

He dropped the knife which clattered to the tiles. Let go his hold on the woman, who spilled down after it in a heap of dead flesh, turned towards the window and began to run.

"No. No. No!!!"

The men moved forward as one, knowing his intent just as surely as he did.

But bargaining was pointless.

They could do little more than watch as he forced his way through the balcony door, flung himself from the 33rd floor and left the world without further thought or explanation as to the overkill kitchen crime splattered all over the tiled floor behind him.

The Carstens, the night of

A scream in the night began it.

There is no godly reason for a telephone to ring at 2.00am.

"Gabriel!"

Vivien Carsten jolted out of her sleep to the shrill piercing cry of the landline, automatically calling her son's name in a half gasp half prayer to either God, or her husband Oliver, as he fought through the tangle of blankets to answer.

Her rapid breathing intensified as she watched his back, the slight nod of his bent head, telephone receiver gripped so tightly in his hand, the flesh of his knuckles turned bony white under the moonlight.

The room breathed with her, a low pulsating throb, every modern gadget and advanced system dutifully running with utter efficiency, letting them know they were doing their job, keeping them, warm, or keeping them cool, keeping some out, keeping them in, keeping them safe. The kind of safety only money can bring. Money can keep out the burglar and murderer and rapist. Money can keep a family safe from harm. Safe from everything . . . but fate.

"Gabriel."

She said his name once more, stupidly, *uselessly*, to her husband's back, in a voice close to tears.

He reached back with a hand to silence her and continued his attentive nodding.

She held her breath and the Carsten house returned to its stillness. A house kept calm by its silence.

He was nineteen now. No longer a child. But try as she might she simply could not see him as a man.

He'd gone out that night, to a club with his friends, and nonchalantly mentioned that he might be back, or might stay at Reece's. Kissing her on the cheek and leaving her to the agony of a mother waiting all night for her child to return from a city as cruel as the sea.

They'd nearly lost him less than a year earlier.

On the Thursday he'd complained of a headache. They'd worried and discussed it at length. He was their only child, and Gabriel never complained about anything.

By Friday he's stopped eating and had forgotten the password to his computer. Vivien wanted to call an ambulance then, but Oliver had resisted, mocking her instead. *She'd remember that.*

He resisted even when Gabriel slept through most of Saturday, only waking up to vomit violently. He resisted right until 7.30 Saturday night when Gabriel fitted, eyes rolling back, saliva bubbling from his nose and mouth, head banging violently on their opulent tiled kitchen floor. It would be the first of a set of seizures endured until the ambulance arrived, each one progressively worse, progressively dreadful, as if God were punishing Oliver for his unpanicked indifference. God would not forgive him for that either. *God would remember it too.*

He spent three weeks in hospital.

The doctors couldn't tell them at first whether he'd survive the meningitis. And if he did whether they'd get the same boy back. The same young man. She may have to mourn him even if he lived, *her beautiful, beautiful boy.*

Something changed within them both as their son lay fighting.

Her thoughts were inflamed, and her dreams infected. She calmly pondered how she'd deal with her husband if his choice to wait, to resist and mock her pleas for help, would mean the end of their son. Leaving him wouldn't do it. He loved her. She knew that. But he loved her the way he loved his car. He'd worked hard to achieve it and others admired it. It got him to work and was reliable. On the outside it shone in its silver sagacity and underneath, *baby it purred!* Sad as he'd be if he lost it, he'd find another. He'd replace it.

And she too was as replaceable as a plastic cup.

The Carsten house glittered and gleamed, an architect's dream house. Oliver was an architect and he'd built the house; he'd built their dream. But there was nothing within it that he could not easily substitute. Nothing, other than his son.

If Gabriel died it would be punishment enough. Oliver would know he'd brought about his own son's end through his arrogance and failings, his insistence on his own way over hers. His own way over everything.

She'd stick around and watch him suffer a while. But it wouldn't be for long. He was a coward despite his outer bravado.

She knew him well enough to know he'd mildly nod through the funeral, thank their family and pointless friends for coming, then get in his shiny, easily replaceable silver car and drive straight off the Des Sandes Bridge, his face aghast in horror as the brick wall of water closed in on the windscreen at breakneck speed.

He finished the call and turned to her. His face aghast. Aghast in horror.

Horror of a different kind.

Gabriel, the night of

"What is wrong with you? *What the fuck is wrong with you?*"

He'd never sworn at this father before. Even amid his hysteria his beleaguered mind momentarily paused to wonder what the comeback would be for pushing the man he so dearly loved and so often feared that one step too far.

But Oliver calmly tolerated the barrage of profanity, just as he was calmly tolerating the pummelling of fist blows his son was raining down on his chest.

He deserved them he supposed, children often mature assuming their parents, *their fathers*, to be exempt from the stained flaws of humanity. He expected Gabriel would have reacted the same way if he'd been charged with drunk driving, or shoplifting, or fraud.

Perhaps this was fraud.

The life he'd created for them, the perfect world, the house designed so immaculately it was barely possible to live in it and feel at home. The night had torn a knife through it all, proclaimed it a fallacy. What he'd created was far from perfection. Their house was cracked, the surface broken, his son's faith in him savaged and gone. His son. His only son. But not his only child. Not anymore.

"Alright," Oliver breathed with a soft command in his voice.

Gabriel's own voice was cracking through the strain of his irate shrieking sobs.

It was time to bring this to a close.

Oliver brought his iron hard arms around Gabriel and for a moment it felt as it had nineteen years ago. The first time. When he'd laid his little head against his chest, his body still slippery and wet with amniotic fluid. He'd folded his arms around him like wings, with a silent promise to never let the wickedness of the world breathe anywhere near him. *His beautiful, beautiful boy.*

"Alright," Oliver said again and Gabriel knew it was time to let go. The last of his incensed punches managed to land on his chest, but the imprisoning cage of his father's arms grew tighter and pulled him in. The beat of his father's heart commanding him, with quiet thunder, telling him through ribcage and sinew and walls of flesh. *'Be still now, boy, be still, surrender'.*

"What is wrong with you?" Gabriel begged to know again, but this time in a broken whisper. Then abruptly he sagged and the tears came and raged against his father's shirt.

Chapter Two

Avery, as it began

The girl Avery stood in the middle of a headstone crowded cemetery where the grass cried for breath and felt her new family approach her from behind.

Around her people stood. People, but not mourners.

No one had come to cry for her mother. And no one for the man who had stuck a knife into her twenty-seven times.

A woman held her hand tightly in hers, but not a cousin or an aunt, not a concerned friend of the family or the mother of a school chum. In her other hand she held a clipboard. Business in both hands. A girl in the left, a file on the girl in the right. A file on Avery Miller.

What was to be done about Avery Miller?

What was to be done about Avery?

What indeed?

She'd left her white sock remain bunched down on her right ankle. She was old enough to pull it up.

She was old enough for many things.

Without a mother there to correct the asymmetry, the social worker had made effort to do so, sighing as she held her phone under her chin, her clipboard under her armpit and, without breaking conversation, bent down to un-bunch the offending sock and help unravel its way back up to her knee.

And who may I ask gave you permission to do that miss pretty?

Avery studied the young woman at her sock work, for a moment letting her fuss with the garment, then began swinging her leg. The social worker sighed her irritation, then, quickly remembering what the girl had been through less than a week before, admonished herself, gave her a fleeting little smile and tried once more.

The swing became a kick, hard, direct, and purposeful. A kick with a surprising amount of a power for such a slight eleven-year-old.

How'd you like that miss pretty?

Seemingly not at all. The kick missed the social worker's face by an inch, nearly knocking her black framed Chanel glasses off the tidy little pert nose.

Avery could hear the insistent voice on the social worker's mobile, demanding to know why she'd suddenly silenced.

Avery returned a quick fleeting smile of her own to the social worker's bewildered face, the Chanel glasses now out of position on the tidy nose, magnifying her wide eyes and making them huge, turning her into a gormless unblinking bug in Avery's imagination.

Avery felt the urge to laugh.

Would that be inappropriate?

The black car had just arrived, and a nice man was holding the door open for her with the kindly look of a grandfather on his face. She didn't want him to see her smirking. She let out nothing but a little giggle, lifted herself off the seat and proceeded, one sock up, one down, towards the vehicle that would take her to watch her mother get swallowed up into a big ol' hole in the earthy chewy ground.

Oliver, as it began

He'd been relieved when Gabriel had been born a boy.

Not that boys, he'd come to realise over the last nineteen years, were always easy. But when Vivien, four years after their wedding, had announced the pregnancy, the thought of bringing a girl into the world left him with the papery taste of fear in his mouth, alongside the champagne they cracked open to celebrate with his parents and hers.

He knew why.

He traced it immediately back to the big mistake.

The big mistake.

The mother of all mistakes.

The monster of all fuck ups.

The Grand Poobah of all irreversible mother-fucking monstrous wrongs.

The big old bad boy that sat beside him for years and years, festering like a rotted corpse. Reminding him every time he relaxed, every time he laughed, of what he carried around his neck like a penance.

He had no siblings now. That hadn't always been the case. He'd been one of a set of triplets. The Carsten Triplets or the Carsten Three or the Trio C, just some of the variables by which they'd come to be known. He'd been born slap bang in the middle. Handsome strong fearless Thaddeus 'Tad' at the forefront, shy little Ellie at the back. Oliver, the middleman, separating the two. Keeping them apart. At least that was what he was meant to do.

He was a man made up of his errors.

He'd always thought 'the big one', the monster, the rotted corpse of all his wrongs would be the one to come back and bite him first. But no, his more recent of misdemeanours, the one made eleven years nine months ago was facing him now, or rather facing away, staring solemnly down at her mother's grave, her hand gripped tightly by a woman in a black suit with tidy hair pinned up in a French twist.

He was given nothing but the back of her head to consider as he trod a careful pathway through the maze of headstones towards her. Two blonde plaits pinned up atop her head, loose baby hair unfettered and free, dancing in the breeze at the nape of a tiny slender pale neck.

The wind around him seemed to know what was coming and the shape it would take.

He'd seen the girl's mother from behind for the first time too. Fallen almost instantly in love with the sight of her golden back. It was a work seminar. He'd made the obligatory statement to Vivien about how much he hated being away from her and Gabe overnight. Kissed her. She'd barely noticed, let alone returned his kiss with anything resembling warmth.

He'd stood and watched his wife without her realising before he left via the back kitchen door.

She was engrossed in something on her laptop. As he'd watched her, she had swung one leg up and rested her right ankle on her left knee. It was a habit of hers, manlike, and unique, he'd always found it curiously erotic, even when she unintentionally let a little fart out in the process.

She farted now, twice, and he itched to pick up the nearest wine bottle and cave the back of her head in.

He thought of saying her name, repeating his goodbyes, see if she'd seem embarrassed, she if she'd even notice.

He chose to do neither and left for the comfort of his car.

The woman had been sitting at a bar in a turquoise backless dress the first time he saw her, it was cut so low he craned his neck, while chatting to work colleagues, to see if he could get any angle in on arse cleavage. A colleague laughed, the complicity sat between them, he'd been trying the very same thing all evening.

They fucked four times that night. He and Vivien hadn't embarked on such a marathon since their twenties. He was lucky if it was four times a week just lately.

Before he left, he sat on the hotel chair in her room and watched her sleeping. Her legs were widely parted, her pussy open, glistening, coated with her own dirty wetness and recent traces of his.

He could still smell her on his fingers, all through the drive home, stopping occasionally, to deeply breathe in her scent.

Thoughts of her consumed him.

He parked at a service station, went to the men's room and found a clandestine cubicle, licking his fingers, begging for the taste of her while he squeezed and jerked his cock with his other hand. He could hear a drunk coughing and belching in the stall next door. It didn't matter. It was a continuation of it all, filthy, illicit, rotten, and wrong. And a spell he didn't want broken just yet.

Seeing Vivien, touching her, that would break it. Bleach it clean. From his fingers, from his mind, from his skin. He crushed thoughts of Vivien out of his head, squeezed himself, almost punishingly and brought himself to a spasming climax, echoing the sounds of the drunk's groans as he squeezed out a turd in the stool next door.

And now it was memories of the woman he strove to crush from his mind, as he we wound his way towards their child. The child he never knew he had, not until the previous night.

He couldn't account for why she hadn't told him. She'd known his name, his company, his details, he wouldn't have been hard to locate.

Maybe she'd longed for child and spent many a night in backless dresses luring in the out-of-town horse studs to impregnate her. Maybe she'd been with someone, as he had, and couldn't risk the life she had. Maybe she was that rarest of creatures, one who wanted nothing from no one and would manage the burden alone.

A burden which now stood at four foot 6 inches tall in a tatty black pinafore dress, scruffy old Mary-Jane shoes with one sock pulled up under her knee and one bunched down at her ankle.

Suddenly, without warning or hesitation she turned to him, as if the wind had reached through him and tapped her shoulder, beckoning her eyes his way.

Those eyes.

They found him like magnets, blue, aching and encumbered with endless sorrow.

She found him.

There in the crowd. As if she knew him. Cells he'd created, parts that were once him, locking in on where they once belonged, finding home in this forest of a world.

Oliver gasped and wondered how he'd ever be able to breathe again.

It was the same as the moment the woman in the backless turquoise dress, her mother, turned to look his way.

Exhilarating, magical, dangerous, life changing, terrifying.

Once again, he fell utterly in love.

Vivien, as it began

She'd been relieved when Gabriel had been born a boy.

Women had never taken to her, nor her to them.

It was probably jealousy. Everyone had said it, her father, her brothers. Evan Tia.

Lovely Tia, slightly mad, self-proclaimed psychic, and her only friend. Probably a lesbian and probably always a little bit in love with her. But she couldn't imagine life without her any more than she could without Gabriel. There was something about a woman who loved her for her beauty rather than resented her for it that she needed in life.

She often mildly wondered if it ever came to saving the three of them from a burning building in which order proceedings would go.

Gabriel first, of course. No point in consideration of any other alternative.

But could she get through life without someone she could really talk to? Be herself with utterly and completely, the way she could with Tia?

Oliver was her partner, her husband, the father of her only child. But she was never allowed to let the act of being the perfect wife slip. Life in that role could be thankless and exhausting.

She stood back and watched him approach the new little bastard thing.

For Christ's sake she was eleven years old. Did she think anyone was buying the *'I'm just too young and clueless to pull my little sock up'* act?

Hopefully she'd be as ugly as the pinafore dress two sizes too big for her she was swanning around in.

Come on, turn round bitchling, show mama a face like a horse.

Oh Fuck.

She was beautiful.

Gabriel, as it began

He'd been relieved to hear his newly announced sibling was a girl.

He'd never had a jealous heart. But maybe that was purely because he'd never had to contend with sibling rivalry before.

At nineteen he'd never quite become the man's man he secretly feared his father had always wanted for a son.

Sharing his father's devotion with another was one thing. Having to share it with a robust rambunctious football mad eleven-year-old oik would be another. A fresh start and new opportunity for his father to have the rough and tough, shake and bake of a chip off the old block he'd always wanted would have been more than his stomach could handle right now.

Perhaps he could content with a girl. How much trouble could she be?

Little flouncy bows and pretty pink dresses; surely no threat? He'd rather get down on his knees on a carpet and play with dolls if he had to, than roll around in the dirt on a rugby pitch pretending he was better at sports than some ragtag eleven-year-old urchin that would probably squeeze his balls or bite his ankles just to show them all who was boss.

She was sitting next to him on the back seat of his father's . . . *their father's* . . . car. Sitting next to him and staring solemnly out of the window, little patches of her breath leaving steamy patterns on the glass as the newly formed Carsten-Miller family drove silently towards some horrendous and impossible future.

He knew his mother felt it the worst. She could never hide her emotions, even her tight shallow breathing seemed to be whispering 'fuck you' to her husband on every curt inward sniff.

Oliver, meanwhile, was fidgeting like a man about to explode with dysentery. Practically every five seconds his eyes would fly around his head like ball bearings in a pin ball machine. To the road, to his wife, to his son, to the eleven-year-old illegitimate daughter none of them had known about until the middle of the previous night, back to the road, back to his wife, back to his son. It was as if he was waiting for the moment the ear crushing tension would break and the three of them would turn like yapping hyenas and tear each other to shreds.

Despite the situation Gabriel wanted to laugh. He'd never seen his father quite so agitated before. Mr perfect with a handle on everything, never a hair or a file or a piece of overpriced furniture even a millimetre out of place.

Guess this one outranks the great mistake, the monster of all fuck ups, daddy-o!

Gabriel had felt his father's love in its purest form the night before. He'd shown him love as he never had in nineteen years, even amid the chaos, the insanity.

His phone had rung about a thousand times. His mother always rang when he was out, begging him to text, just to let her know he was ok. It was sweet but overbearing. But this time the insistence had been impossible to ignore, and he'd drunkenly stumbled outside the club to see what the fuss was about.
That fuss that now sat next to him silently steaming up patches on the car windows like a little cocker spaniel.

After the inevitable emotional fallout his father had held him, calmed in, with a strength that was warrior-like and overwhelming. He'd then wrapped him in a blanked and put a hot chocolate in front of him in the quiet blue lights of their kitchen and waited patiently until his son found a way to speak?

"Do you love her?"

Gabriel had studied his father, watched him shake his head piteously before answering. "It was eleven years ago Gabe. One night. I love your mother. I slipped."

"No. The girl. Do you love her?" Gabriel asked the question but wasn't sure he wanted to hear the answer.

"I've never even met her. Until tonight I didn't even know she existed."

Non-committal. Hmmm. Coward's way out.

Oliver had gotten up then, nodded at the untouched hot chocolate in front of his son. "Drink that and try to get some sleep."

Gabriel's pain laced voice stopped his father at the kitchen door. "Dad,"

Oliver turned to him.

"Do you love me?"

'Oh Gabe', his eyes had said, his heart too broken, his voice too close to tears to be able to answer.

Answer him! Tell him! *'I love you deeply, utterly, profoundly. I love you more than life. Without you there is no life.'*

"Turn out the lights before you come to bed." His warrior father chose to say to him instead and left him alone to his hot chocolate and another round of tears.

Martin Black snr, as it began

He spied the silly little thing sitting in the back of the silver Mercedes and pondered the best way to get at it.

He could step out in front of the car, let them swerve to the right, hit a tree. They'd catch blood dripping from cracked open foreheads in their hands as they came round dazed and dreamlike, stare at it aghast, not knowing what had happened, only realising too late when the car burst into flames and engulfed them.

But they seemed a nice family, especially the young lad who'd held the door open for him at the foster home. They didn't deserve such a fate.

It didn't either. It deserved something far more befitting. He preferred it to die slowly.

Thin, clouds formed above him, their shadows lengthening out. Spring was too mellow a season to hold the hell in his heart. This day deserved the fiendish breath of summer, summer from a desert, fierce and unforgiving, where the shrubs choke and the carcasses of dead animals litter the highways, their bones poking through broken skin like springs through fraying furniture. A ripe time for vultures, for maggots, for worms. Summer's hell under a devil's hot sun.

He smiled a gaunt mean smile with teeth so yellow they seemed painted with poison and launched himself at the silver car, his face smashing against the window where it sat.

They all jumped, and the man instinctively slammed on his breaks, throwing his head around to stare at the sudden intrusion, befuddled and disbelieving.

Martin Black senior wiped his face all over the window like a sponge, leaving smears of sweat and drooling saliva across the glass.

The woman inside was demanding something, probably that her husband drive away.

He was scrambling to do just that, panicking, trying to find first gear.

It shrieked at the sight of him and cowered back, into the lap of the nice young man who'd held open the door and unbeknownst to him, let him near it. Now it was trying to bury itself in his chest, burrow into his skin as if to find some hole to hide in.

The woman was shrieking and grabbing for her phone. The man was coming to his senses. They'd be gone soon; he'd miss his chance.

Bash, bash bash.

The cement brick hit the window three times before it broke, raining in on them in a shower of glass.

It screamed and tried to burrow itself further into the young man's skin.

Don't play possum with me! Leave innocence to the innocent. It's you and me now. Toe to toe!

"I just want to talk to her, okay?" He offered to the frantic couple in the front of the car, before turning to it, his face contorting with rage.

"Why did you do it!!!?"

"Dad, drive away! For fuck sake, drive away!" the nice young man was shrieking at his father, while trying to prize its arms from round his neck so he could breath.

The man nodded at his son over his shoulder and tried to do just that. But shock and fear were making him as useless as a great baby and he could only stab at the breaks rather than hit the gas.

"Why did you do it!!!?" He thundered.

The man would find his senses soon and they'd be gone. As nice as the young man was, he wouldn't be holding the door open for him again any time soon, certainly not into a marvellous house the likes of which would have such a sleek silver Mercedes sitting in the drive.

His eyes glowed an angry inflamed orange and he launched himself through the broken window, grabbing for it. He got a hold, he had it, a handful of hair and a fistful of tatty pinafore dress. He could pull back now and take it with him. Lumber away with it, stuff it into a sleeping bag also filled with rocks and stones, throw it far off into a river and give it to a watery grave. But witches don't drown, do they? *He'd think of something of else.*

The pain shot up his nose like a bullet from a gun.

The force of it made him throw his head up and face a benevolent sky.

Had it kicked him? No. It was still squirming and struggling and trying to fight its way into the boy's insides.

It was him. *Oh nice young man, now really?*

There was blood on both their faces. His blood. The young man had pushed her away long enough to bring his head back and thrust it at him like a footballer heading a ball towards the goal at Wembley.

His nose had broken immediately with a sickening crack.

Senses returned, the man had finally found first gear and off they tore, through the country lane away, away and away.

He wobbled once, like a drunk, watching them leave as he raged. He tried to repeat his question *'Why did you do it?'* But his mouth was filling with blood and all he spurted was a babble of incoherent yawps.

"Wiiiiiieee 'id ou d'it? Whyyyyyyy 'idou dooooit?"

The clouds above him broke apart, answering his fury with slowly shifting whiteness that parted and let through beams of gentle yellow sunlight, promising a summer that may still come. A summer that would be born of the devil, if only he'd find a way to swerve the angles of God.

The blood that pulsed from his face turned black and soon he tumbled into a world of darkness. Darkness for a time was the answer, darkness was peace, darkness was enough, darkness was good.

Even though, like light, like summer and spring, darkness never lasted, not for very long.

Detective McNally, as it began

Gabriel jerked his head away from his mother's fussing hands as she, for the fourth time that hour, tried to examine his face for any signs of damage or injury following his recent act of heroism. Unconcerned about any facial trauma, Gabriel was far more interested in the tall enigmatic detective who was standing in their kitchen, laying pictures of their recent assailant and his deceased son out on the table.

"I'm sorry you had to experience that," Detective McNally began.

Oliver was leaning against the window frame, watching Avery outside, turning slow sad circles on the small brightly painted merry-go-round, the social worker barely engaged in the depressing little game, one hand on the handle, the other, and all her attention, on her mobile phone.

"Who the hell was it?" Oliver asked without taking his eyes off his newly acquired daughter.

"Martin Black senior." McNally answered, lining pictures of father and son side by side on the table. "Father of her mother's killer."

"Christ haven't that family put her through enough?" Said Oliver.

"I don't think he wanted to hurt her. I don't think the man knows what he wants. He's half mad with grief. He lost his wife and daughter in a car crash a year ago. And now this."

Oliver only sighed, his eyes still fixed on the child he'd never known, imagining what the short years of her life had already put her through.

"Mr Carsten," said McNally "I'd advise changing your locks, your email and house security codes, also your telephone lines. Land and mobile."

"Will he come after her again?" asked Vivien, her protective eyes immediately flying to Gabriel, rather than the girl at the route of her question.

"He'll be sectioned no doubt." McNally answered. "It's more press intrusion that concerns me. They're insidious little parasites at the best of times. But when it's a murder case like this, especially involving a child, can be months before they get their teeth out of your skin."

"Detective," Vivien said, almost guiltily.

Oliver sighed, knowing what was coming next.

"We have a gun in the house." Vivien went on. "It's perfectly legal. We built this house on a farm we inherited from my parents. We inherited the gun along with it and have the correct licence. We keep it in the bedroom."

"Do you have a code on the lock?" asked McNally.

"Gabriel's nineteen." Vivien answered, the guilt in her voice ratcheting up several notches.

"Put one on, please, this evening." Instructed McNally.

Vivien looked over to nod her agreement to McNally and instruction to Oliver, only to find the fleeting image of the back of his shirt as he left the kitchen and appeared through the frame of the window, heading towards the new little bitchling.

She crossed their opulent tiles and took up the same position Oliver had recently vacated and watched him coldly as he reached her.

"Why would he do it?" It was Gabriel, studying the pictures on the tabletop with intense questioning eyes.

"We all need someone to blame." Vivien answered, her eyes homing in on Avery Miller.

"No, his son. Her stepfather. Why would he do that?" Gabriel asked picking up the picture of the late Martin Black junior.

"It's happened all too often before I'm afraid son." Detective McNally volunteered as he began packing up the photographs and other items. "A couple live together happily for forty years. Then suddenly it'll end in murder over what one of them wants to watch on television. Strangers, get in a row, over a parking space, one pulls a knife."

Vivien turned back from the window.

"By all accounts he was a quiet decent man." McNally added. "Restrained."

"Restrained?" Gabriel queried incredulously.

McNally clicked his briefcase shut and looked at him earnestly. "Each man has his limit. Some people are born bad. Some are made so by years of systematic abuse. And some, for one crazy moment, just slip. They say inside every human heart a quiet killer sleeps."

Father and Daughter, as it began

The brightly coloured merry-go-round carried Avery Miller round in slow sombre circles. She gazed at the moving flashes of grass as she passed them, staring forlornly ahead with eyes so blue they may as well have swallowed the pale cold moon.

Oliver reached the merry-go-round and nodded at the social worker, his eyes asking for privacy. Without breaking the flow of her conversation, the social worker gladly relinquished her efforts with the merry-go-round and retreated to her car.

Oliver pushed the handle, letting Avery pass him three times before suddenly gripping the wood and bringing the ride to a sudden stop.

She turned her huge eyes his way.

"I know how hard this must be for you." He felt clumsy, ridiculous, a fraud just for talking to her, as nervous as a teenager asking out a girl for the first time.

She stared at him, eyes like marbles in the day's fading light.

"I'm going to do my best to give you a home . . . and a family."

He bent down, un-bunched her fallen sock and slowly fed it back up her leg to sit under her tiny knee.

"No one will ever hurt you again."

She sat, caught in the pull of his gaze, cells and bones and tissue, all that comprised her, suddenly glimpsing the source of its existence, blood smelling the blood from which it had first sprang, skin knowing the nearness of itself, itself encasing another human soul.

He searched her eyes deeply, as if trying to scan the interiors of her brain.

Was she registering his words? Did she believe them to be true?

Or simply not give a shit?

He'd had passion for his wife once. Now, simply respect for her. He'd known love for his son. Love he would kill or die for.

This, this half born, fledging thing, this feeling that pushed him across a tightrope like a gun in his back, this was removing every bit of order he'd used to brick up the fireplace of his vulnerability.

She studied him in the cool light, making him feel as though he should apologize for spanking her. Then dug her scuffed shoes into the gravel and pushed herself away to spin in slow circles, round and round on the coloured wood.

What squeezed the tender spaces around his heart was vague and unknowable. Her eyes trailed the earth as she passed him and yet he felt scrutinised, examined, a frog pinned to a board awaiting vivisection.

He stood up and saw his wife in the framed window, silent and still, like a ghost caught in an old photograph, hiding behind the wooden slats and her tumble of black curls. The eyes that peered and probed and unapologetically pointed his way, of course, were hers.

Husband and Wife, as it began

She'd given him little more than the back of her head, the coldness of her shoulder, since they'd been back that day.

He was happy not to try to kiss her, or make amends, or appease her, or go through all the little hells of banishment and silence but knew these were the marks of death for a marriage already teetering on the edge of the bucket under a noose.

She was always a woman to forget what she chose to and remember everything she wanted to.

There was little point at this stage in him trying to play the game. If he got it right, he'd be wrong, if he got it wrong, she'd be right. Someone might as well have shackled them together blindfolded with a knife in each hand, settling it all that way would have been fairer and far less bloody.

His ice-cold wife kept firmly turned away, illuminated in a glow of lamplight that made him want to run his hand over the skin of her arm. Why did he always want whatever he was denied. He could feel vibrations coming from deep within her stone-cold limbs, as if her soul were Imprisoned there, desperately struggling to be let out, reach him, fall into his arms, beg like a child for him to make it all go away.

There was one thing at least they both knew had to happen.

"Avery." Vivien said and it was as if the word meant murder. "How sweet."

He'd had to think of a code for the gun case. Normally their passwords were always 'Gabriel-Mark'.

It wasn't always easy having a witch for a wife. He was sure the damn woman could see through walls. How she'd managed to catch a glimpse of the password he had programmed into the gun case god only knew.

"How long are you going to keep punishing me?" he asked and put the gun case back on the top shelf of their wardrobe.

He slid into bed beside her, accompanied only by her silence.

A framed picture of Gabriel sat on the table next to his side of the bed. He picked it up and slid his thumb across the image of Gabriel's cheek.

"Bang on the devil's door and he'll smack your head right through the window." Vivien said without turning round.

Something was better than nothing. He returned the photo to the table and turned back to her.

"When Gabriel was in hospital last year with meningitis," Oliver said "I got down on my knees like I was ready to cut a deal with God. Like it was a used car I was bargaining for, or a piece of real estate. 'Let me have him a while longer, and you can take him another time, even when he's still young; thirty, twenty-two, even next week. Just let me have him long enough to open his eyes and look at me, even if only one more time.' My beautiful, beautiful boy."

Oliver sighed and slid further down in the bed, closing his eyes, even if the possibility of sleep was as remote as the moon.

"Bet they're laughing at me now." He whispered.

"Who?"

His eyes came open at the sound of her voice.

"The devil," said Oliver "and God. At the silly little man down on bended knees."

He looked at the back of her head. She returned him nothing more than stiff silence.

She edged away and kept her face deep in her pillow as he reached over her to turn off the light, lest he see her face and know that she had been weeping.

The phone rang at close to two a.m. that morning.

Almost the same time it had pieced through the night a mere twenty-four hours earlier. A call to have pierced through the night and then their lives. Alerting him to the death of an erstwhile one-night stand and the existence of a daughter never known, never considered.

Mary Miller had made it clear in letters kept among her personal effects who the little girl's father was and how, in the event of her death, he could be contacted. And yet there was no evidence of illness, no notes about internal organ maladies, no signs, or even tests for cancer of any kind.

Yet cancer had teeth and could snarl and bite.

Mary Miller had known a different malignancy was chewing on her insides, felt the spread of it, foreshadowing her own, perhaps both, or all three of their deaths. A cancer that moved in and made promises of love and ate with her and slept with her and paid half the bills and played husband and stepfather a while. Then with the malevolent finality of all unstoppable parasites, took a total of twenty-seven bites out of her fine soft flesh.

And that, as they say, was that.

What was to be done about Avery Miller?

What was to be done about Avery?

What indeed?

Mr Carsten, if you'd be so kind as to pick up daddy duties from here.

It'll be just like having a new kitchen installed, a fresh little start for you and your family to love and enjoy as the years roll in.

He turned to Vivien to see if the call had woken her, but she was snoring lightly and sleeping deeply.

She wouldn't have heard it anyway.

34

The phone was only ringing down deep in the layers of his soul. Down in the blackness of his own drooling dream sleep, his answerless imagination.

Down in the dark-dream-ribbons that laced through his fitful frantic snatches of sleep. Down where the slumber wolves lurk and lick and snap, roam, stare with yellow eyes, circle and wait, just to remind a man of all his fears.

The pack of Oliver-dream-wolves threw back their large heads in unison, lifting their furry muzzles to howl at a wickedly white moon. Howls that merged and once fully fused were the sound of a telephone's persistently shrill ringing cry.

He sat up in his dream world to answer.

'Ellie, it's been so long since you called me like this.'

The gurgling sound her voice made because she was no longer able to swallow or cough, letting saliva build up in the back of her throat and upper airways, made Oliver constrict with sickly unease.

'Oliver, Oliver my brother.'

Her death rattle had grown stronger and more abhorrent over the years.

He opened his eyes and saw her, sitting comfortably at the foot of the bed, telephone in one hand up to hole in the side of her head where once an ear had been. With her other hand she reached out and stroked the length of Vivien's shin, the peeling skin stretching like tattered lace over her skeletal arm flaked generously, showering skin-snow down onto their bed clothes.

Oliver kept the phone up to his own ear, even though she was no more than three feet away.

'Ellie, why have you called, why have you come?'

'Remember Oliver, remember the great mistake, the monster of all fuck ups, the Grand Poobah of all irreversible mother fucking colossal wrongs.'

It was a long sentence to come rattling out of the throat of a dead woman. She coughed slightly with the strain of it and grey blood grew and lengthened through long neglected veins, sitting like a forgotten network under the skin of her sucken cheeks.

'Don't tell me this is worse.'

Vivien stirred slightly. Oliver held his breath and clutched the imagined phone receiver tight to his chest. She'd heard his delirium sleep babble chats with Ellie once before. Years earlier. The night after the time, *the only time*, he'd hit Gabriel.

Father and son had kept the event hidden from her and promised to forgive each other and never speak of it again.

But the dream-wolves had sucken their teeth right in like it was a big juicy just-slaughtered steak and Ellie had been sure to phone that night and remind him then of all his wrongs, and the way, try as you might, you can never box them up and put them away. Those wrongs come together and form something, something that has a way of seeping through the world around you, sluggish and filthy, staining whatever it touched.

Vivien had asked him the next morning what all the sleep talk had been about? Some sort of great mistake, and a Poobah of a fuck up. She'd laughed as she'd asked.

"I reversed the car into a tree." He lied. It was being MOT'd and he was currently driving a courtesy Nissan Micra; she'd never know the difference.

She'd laughed again. "No wonder you were having nightmares." And continued searching for the Witch Hazel to dab on the bruise under her son's eye from the fall he'd had trying to skateboard the day before. She'd told Oliver not to buy him a skateboard that Christmas, he was never a lad into such things, and try as he might

Oliver would never carve and shape their son into something he wasn't. *Oliver, Oliver, Oliver*, never one to learn. No matter how many mistakes he made.

'Tell me.'

He begged his sister and watched as she pulled the knotted white bed sheet away from her throat. The spinal cord transection that had occurred when she hanged herself mercifully meant that death was instant, but left her neck with no infrastructure to support itself or carry her skull, even in her current rotted-corpse manifestation, loosening her noose a little let her words come easier despite the persistence of her death rattle drum, but made her head loll to one side like a doll that had lost its stuffing.

'Oliver my brother, just watch what you let into this house.'

"Please don't call me anymore Ellie." He begged her in a voice that had managed to escape through the prison of his sleep, and sensed Vivien murmur a response in what may have been the cages of her own dark dreams.

'You go now Ellie.'

'Why Oliver, why brother?' She rattled and croaked.

'Because you're dead.'

The parting click of the receiver and the flat dull tone of the line met him instantly.

He turned over in bed and laid his arm round his wife's waist, buried his faced in her curls, breathed her in, desperate for the nearness of something warm, something real.

After an aching minute she rolled over and held him.

Chapter Three

Father and Son, the first day

He deliberately skirted his parents' open bedroom doorway, trotting across the sand smooth carpet of the lesser used back stairs, hoping to be unnoticed, so he could escape the house and the tension that had been simmering therein since the *'joy'* of the new arrival.

"Gabe!"

His father's voice was like a fist, grabbing hold of a handful of shirt and yanking him back.

Gabriel sighed, reluctantly turning on the top step to face him.

"I'm on my way out." Gabriel offered before his father had a chance to suggest otherwise.

"Not tonight you're not." Oliver said without hesitation as he reached him, oblivious, or ignoring, his son's rolling eyes. "There's twenty quid on the dresser. Get a pizza for you and your sister."

"For me and my *what?*"

It was a more daringly sarcastic tone than he would normally adopt for his father. He'd had free licence in the last day or two, riding on the coattails of his father's latest 'great mistake'. But things were acclimatising now, and the usual strict order of dominance was returning. Everyone knew his or her place and position in the Carsten household and Gabriel only had free rein for the superiority of the wronged over the wrongdoer for so long. The great alpha male, the big gorilla, the daddy bear, was raising angry eyes and showing him the first flashes of a warning stare.

"I've got plans, I'm going out with Reece." Gabriel said, trying to hide the weakness of intimidation in his voice.

Oliver shook his head. "I'm taking your mother out to dinner. I need you to babysit."

"I'm going out with-"

"Gabe!"

"What am I supposed to do with her?"

"I don't know. Play with her."

"*Play with her?*"

"You're spending too much time with that jackass anyway. Get in trouble whenever you're with him you do. You start university in Autumn, and I don't want you screwing anything up for yourself."

"What am I going to screw up?"

"You're a kid still. You don't understand. This world isn't a kind place. You make one little mistake, and you could destroy everything." Oliver turned away from his son, tucking his shirt into his trouser belt line. "The tiniest slip could come back to haunt you Gabe."

"When? In eleven years, nine months like yours did?"

Yeah, take that daddy-o. You're not going to make me feel like shit over this. You hypocrite, you stranger-fucker, your illegitimate daughter-maker, you wandering dick.

Oliver turned sharply back like a dog, snarling from his flank as if stung by a bee.

"Gabriel, you cannot afford to be this selfish. You are not my only child anymore."

"Was I ever?"

Don't push me child. I may not own you. But you be sure I made you. And if I ever needed to, I'd remind you who owns this house.

"Boy one day your hour will come."

He said it with a cool and even tone, eyes locked in on his son as though he'd gone momentarily insane. It had been as quick and as brutal as an open fisted slap and stung with as much cruelty.

Oliver immediately wanted to snatch it back, to gobble the words up from the air, swallow them back down his throat. But they were there, settled in the permanent, in the enduring, the unforgivable, lodged in Gabriel's heart, the way three years earlier the welt of a fulsome lump lodged around his eye, soon to turn yellow, ringed by a more beauteous damson, handiwork of his father's momentary slip of monstrous rage.

He'd forgiven him for it. His father had asked, begged, cried. Gabriel had agreed, agreed, agreed.

It's nothing, I'm ok, it doesn't matter, not at all.

But his father didn't ask for forgiveness, not this time, he simply stared at his son like a stranger.

It's everything, I'm not ok, it matters, I love you daddy, but why would you hurt me, why would you kill the love between us, why would you kill me like this?

Gabriel was the one to turn away, lest his father see the first trace of tears that were prickling in his eyes.

Reece, The first day

What a prick!

His best friend clearly wasn't in the mood for games.

Sitting sulkily at one end of the couch while this new *'sister thing'* he was expecting him to understand sat just as sulkily at the other, playing morosely with some tatty rag doll piece of crap and swinging her leg so violently it came within an inch of smashing into the overpriced glass coffee table on every upwards kick. Vivien Carsten would need an hour in a decompression unit if she'd been there to see that little act of petulant defiance.

He thought about a joke to lighten the mood.

Gabe, did you know the city is holding their annual incest competition this weekend? I've entered my sister.

Hmmm . . .

Maybe not.

He'd need to find another way to amuse himself.

He fished in his bag, soon retrieving two large books and setting them *'oh so nonchalantly'* down on the coffee table in front of his pal.

Gabriel picked up the top book and read the title. "The Study of Occult Practises"

Score, he'd taken the bait.

Even the little sister thing took interest, putting down the time-chewed doll and edging closer to them both, pushing a few strands of unkempt hair out of her eyes as she looked at the picture on the cover of the second book which Gabriel was now holding.

Jesus, those eyes. He hadn't noticed just how pretty the little girl was until now.

"Magic, Alchemy and Extra Sensory Perception." Gabriel slapped down the book and turned angrily to Reece. "Are you kidding? My dad will kill me."

Reece held a finger up to silence him, delved deeper into the bag and returned with the main event.

He placed a large triangular wooden device proudly atop the table in front of them.

The girl's interest grew, she was edging closer still, big pretty eyes alive with interest, the tatty doll discarded face down on the cushion, childhood games were over.

Gabriel flipped through the book and landed on a black and white illustration of a similar device. Reece had earmarked the page heavily and the book opened appropriately to present the illustration like an invitation. Within the illustration a group of five sat around a similar triangular box, two touching its long central dial. The other three participants looked terrified over their shoulders, seeing a muscular horned demon step out through the shadows to bear down on them.

Reece grinned and nodded at the device.

Gabriel's face contorted in incredulous irritation.

"He told you to play with her." said Reece defensively.

"I don't think '*in the realms of the occult*' is what he had in mind." answered Gabriel and read angrily from the inscription under the illustration. "Players should proceed with caution for not only can their intrusions into the spiritual world disturb the peace of any incorporeal or immaterial being, it can also make manifest more false and ungodly malevolent paranormal demons or fallen angels, with a want to tempt humans to sin, up to the one entity which is

42

known as the personification of all evil and the devout enemy of humankind and God himself."

Gabriel snapped the book shut and tossed it aside, shaking his head at Reece.

From nowhere Avery was suddenly in his lap, as unannounced and uninvited as she had been when she arrived in it in the car after her mother's funeral when the half mad Martin Black senior had attacked, albeit without the frantic fear for her life and shrieking panicked hysteria.

Gabriel had never known what it was to have a sibling. Reece was as close as it had ever come. He felt a bond of brotherhood with his friend, would have fought for him, done anything for him, helped him however he asked. But something felt strange and new as the little girl settled on top of him and made herself at home. The softness of the back of her head resting gently on his shoulder, silky little legs with hardly any weight to them at all, laying across his own with the warmth of a blanket.

It could only have been his imagination, but somewhere deep inside, cylinders seemed to be firing, nerves alerted, near dead cells that had reached their cycle's end, suddenly bursting with life like buds in spring, as if their other halves had arrived and were calling them home.

I found you. I found you. I found you.

So thumped the beat of his heart.

He had assumed he would find her irritating, an inconvenience, a threat, a competitor for his father's attention and affection. He wasn't expecting this. He wasn't expecting to feel like an amputee who'd suddenly regained his arms. He wasn't expecting this strange, instantaneous, inexplicable feeling.

He folded his arms over her like gates that would protect her from the world.

He hadn't expected this to feel so natural, so right.

He hadn't planned for love.

Reece did a small double take at the impromptu act of sibling solidarity, felt a tiny squeeze of jealousy pinch his heart.

Whatever. He'll be bored by the time she gets her first period.

He pushed the triangular device towards them on the table. To the right of the dial was a scrawled word YES. On the left a neighbouring NO.

"Look, you ask it things." Reece said.

He held the dial with the tip of his index finger and drew it to the far right.

"Is my name Reece?" he closed his eyes and asked it.

He let go, freeing the dial which swung with elegant ease to the left, back to the right, left right, left right left, finally settling on the right side and the firm answer YES.

"See now you try." He said, pushing the box an inch closer to Gabriel.

"I think I know my own name."

"Ask it something else." Reece insisted.

Gabriel anchored his left arm round Avery like a seatbelt to stop her sliding off his lap, leant forward and pulled back the dial. "Is Reece a dickhead?"

With six swings, and to his great satisfaction, the dial landed squarely back on the world YES.

"It does work." Said Gabriel causing Avery to laugh.

The cylinders fired again. Her laugh was like melting butter. It was the first time he'd heard it. The first time he'd heard anything from her other than the startled screams of a child cowering from a man-monster.

Reece tutted his annoyance. "The only way we can really test it is by getting someone we don't know all that well to ask it something."

Gabriel stared blankly at him, before suddenly realising what he had in mind.

"No way!" Gabriel barked and instinctively tightened his hold on the little girl in his lap.

Reece looked at him, quietly asking with his eyes.

Soon she swivelled round in his arms and turned her eyes on him too. Eyes that asked the same. *'Come on, let's play.'*

Jesus, those eyes. They could carve up a man's heart. Make the moon break its moorings and lose its grip on the tides.

Gabriel tore himself out of their magnetic pull and scowled at them both. "No!"

Avery, the first day

He held her hand in his hand and she felt like she could conquer the world.

I found you. I found you. I found you.

So thumped the beat of her heart.

I was cold, and tired, this ol' world left me sick and sad.

I tried loving once, but all it left was calluses, scar tissue all over my hands and heart. Dead brain cells from too much thinking, clogged aortas from too much hoping, twisted vessels from too much trusting, allergic rhinitis inflammation, from holding my breath for far too long, just to make sure I could hear you saying my name.

She didn't need their help to climb on to the seat they were setting up in front of the fireplace. But she would take it anyway. She had climbed on or over several things far bigger than the posh chair with the marble frame and inbuilt silk cushions. She was old enough to conquer that puny height.

She was old enough for many things.

But this new brother of hers, and his idiot friend, held one hand each as though she were a bride marrying them both and half guided, half lifted her up into place.

I found you. I found you. I found you.

So thumped the beat of her heart.

Her new brother still wasn't happy. Didn't like what the fool was suggesting she do. He scowled morosely as fool-boy set the triangle box on the mantle in front of her.

"Now, this is how it works little girl."

46

I'm not three, prick face.

"It doesn't have to be just 'yes' or 'no' answers. You can ask it a question where the answer is a number. And we count how many times it swings."

She nodded dutifully, the way children who have no conviction as to their own authority do. An empty acquiescence. She could have been agreeing to him boiling her like a cabbage.

Her brother was sighing, good. He wanted to keep her safe.

She looked up into his warm soft face.

Finally, reluctantly, he nodded his agreement.

Cautiously, she faced it, it now seemed ominous, threatening, and real. Her tiny finger drew back the long thick needle shaped dial.

"How many nights," Avery began.

She wanted to be clever in front of him. Clever and adult. Not ask the questions of an eleven-year-old. *What age will I marry? How many children will I have one day? Sigh, gosh, isn't she sweet, pink posies and ponies and vomit all over the rug.*

She wanted the question he would hear from her mouth to be one with thick juicy meat and gristle on its bones.

She wanted him to know sugar and spice were the last two things she was made of.

"How many nights," she repeated and felt the whole room hold its breath "before someone dies in this house?"

Neither the boys, nor the girl, nor the room dared to breathe.

Finally, Reece. "Isn't she a sweetheart?"

Gabriel let out a small bubble of slightly disturbed laughter and put his hand over Avery's on the dial to prevent her letting it go. "I can't believe you. You've been in this house three days and not said a word to anyone and when you finally do open your mouth that's the first thing you come out with?"

Avery froze. Was she in trouble? Losing him as soon as she found him?

Then he smiled again. A smile that became a laugh.

Her question was ugly and sour. Like her frayed pinafore dress and her scuffed Mary Jane shoes. But he loved it. He loved it because it was hers.

I found you. I found you. I found you.

She smiled back at him. A smile that followed his and collapsed to laughter. Then they laughed together. The two halves of one whole. Laughing, giggling, smirking in their complicity, while idiot boy scratched his head.

Her brother turned suddenly serious and looked over at prick features. "I'm not having her ask it that. How do we stop it?"

"We can't." twat face told him. "She's gonna have to let go of it. It'll start swinging as soon as she does."

He sighed an angry sigh, and, on his breath, she heard it clearly *'no one messes with my little sister'*.

"What do you care anyway? You don't believe." The fool was asking her brother, asking him, goading him, provoking him.

Watch yourself there bonehead.

He took his hand away from her hand and she felt the loss of his touch from her fingers all the way down to the balls of her feet.

She released her hold on the dial and let it begin its slow rhythmic journey.

Right to left, left to right.

They all followed it fervently with their eyes.

Tick, tick, tick

I found you. I found you. I found you.

Right to left.

Will you braid my hair?

Left to right.

Do you like me?

Tick, tick

Stop.

They stopped with it. Each afraid to move. Afraid to speak. Afraid to look over their shoulders lest a horned demon was crashing its way through the ceiling.

"Seven" confirmed Reece. "Next Saturday."

Something in the house's deeper parts clatter-crashed as if beaten like a drum and the light fizzled and hissed, then failed, engulfing them in abrupt darkness.

Gabriel, the first day

He was frightened but couldn't show it. Maximum bravado was required in front of them.

In front of her.

He was the big brother now. The role required such things as fearlessness and strength. Time to put away childhood games.

Yet as they inched their way in impenetrable darkness along the landing wall towards the hatch to the loft he couldn't help but feel they were playing at some juvenile Scooby-Doo haunted house type escapade.

He swallowed his nerves and thought of what to say. He couldn't be Shaggy, had to be Fred. Fred always had a handle on these situations. What would Fred say?

"Keep back from the edge of the stairs, here, take my hand."

"I'm ok." Reece answered from within the dark.

"Not you, you lame dick!" Gabriel said as he bumped into the door to the airing cupboard and realised they were in the place they needed to be, under the access door that would lead to the attic.

The air in the attic was thick with dust and memories.

Memories of the days leading up to a lifetime of Christmases, clambering up the ladder with his father to retrieve lights, wrapping paper, decorations, an assortment of the season's most magical items.

And memories of the dark days, the bad year, the 'great mistake', the terrible thing.

He wasn't sure why the bullying at school had started.

Tia and his mother did their best to convince him it was because he was special, beautiful. The contempt of his peers born of the bitter cruelty of jealousy.

He lived most of that year alone and miserable, hour long lunchbreaks that stretched out like centuries, friendless and forgotten. Wandering the playground with his hands in his pockets and a heaviness in his heart.

He wasn't the rambunctious, funny, *ok at maths and great at games*, son his father had wanted. He was now the freak, taunted in classrooms, picked last at sports, and never included at social gatherings. Other than the times they asked him to come, only to find he'd been duped, and waited alone on street corners until an hour had passed, to then trudge slowly home, humiliated, lonely and in tears.

Most of the boys from his class were going to a nightclub together when the first of them turned sixteen. He hadn't been invited.

"What if I come and sit and have a drink while you dance?" his mother had offered.

Looking back now he knew it was a suggestion born of sweetness. But at the time he felt a sickly anger towards her that made him want to set her on fire. The torments at school were bad enough. What did she think they'd do to him? A whole pack of them, drunk and wild with the exuberance of youth, suddenly seeing him out on a Friday night with 'mummy'?

But things had changed when Reece took him under his wing.

Reece was unlike them, unlike him, unlike anyone. In the days before the bullying and the 'isolation' he was condemned to, he'd have never considered Reece for a friend. He was an oddball.

51

Erratic, free spirited, devil-may-care. Always scruffy, often smelly, but he looked life right in the face and squeezed something out of every moment of it.

When he befriended the once popular, now loner, Gabriel Carsten things got better almost immediately. He found himself laughing, in a genuine way, and knew a happiness again, perhaps even a more honest and real happiness than that of previous years, brotherly bonds known in a deeper way.

Reece was the youngest of four brother and always had some memento of their lives to share with his friend, music, clothes, alcohol and on that dreadful day, pornography.

He knew his father would have been wild with rage so only agreed if they took the old style disks up to the loft for clandestine viewing.

The first few were hysterical, rather than anything erotic, nail screeching bad acting, and nothing more titillating than what they'd experienced while seeing women sunbathing on the beach. The whole event was a joke. Until they popped in the fourth disk, the one that changed everything.

This brought viewing of a different kind, something that could never be unseen.

They realised the girl was no more than twelve five minutes into the film and even in their own naivety felt sick with shame and the wrongness of it. But by then Oliver was home from work and poking his head through the hatch to the loft to see what they were up to.

His parents had sent Reece home immediately and spent the next hour in the kitchen with Gabriel demanding to know if there was some monstrous part of their son they hadn't been aware of until this day.

He explained it as it was, and his mother took his side almost immediately. But she would have taken his side on anything. If he'd been caught smoking or shoplifting or skipping school. He'd still be her darling boy, her little sweetling.

Her frustration turned from her son to her husband who, two hours on was still refusing to be convinced.

Finally, she persuaded him to take the boy to the park to smooth out their differences and reconnect.

When they got back, she'd been pleased to find they were friends again. Even if Gabriel was sporting a black eye. Why Oliver had bought him that skateboard in the first place, let alone pick that day to encourage Gabriel to try it out again was beyond her. But the accident seemed to have done the trick. Oliver fussed and fretted over him in a way he hadn't since Gabriel was a toddler.

She wasn't happy about the rising lump that was thickening and swelling under her son's eye, but if that was what it took for them to find each other again she would let fate have its way.

A sudden flash of blinding light stole him back from the memory of it all.

He'd fished his camera out of the drawer in his bedroom, set its self-timer and given it to Reece to hold as he'd clambered up the ladder and found his way inside. The circles of white-gold brilliance from the flash giving him quick snatches of light to find his way.

There'd be about a hundred useless pictures he'd have to delete someday, but at least they had gotten him safely inside.

"Take one more!" Gabriel called out and in the ensuing golden flash found the fuse box and pulled the middle switch down, resetting the Carsten house to light and colour and warmth and normalcy.

Normalcy that was, besides what they let in that night, the uninvited guest.

Gabriel wrote the sudden sense that something was watching him off as his fearful imagination.

That strange noise that sounded like breathing, that was nothing more than the gentle hum of their electrical system, slowly waking and coming to life and order again.

That cold chill on the back of his neck, that was nothing more than the last winds of winter, refusing to give way to the promise of spring, finding their way through gaps in the attic roof. All attic rooves have gaps, surely, even in a house as modern and airtight as this.

Cold winds and other elements can find their way into a house, if their gusts are strong enough, their minds are sharp enough, sharp with direction and with intent.

"You forgot the fucking thing!" Gabriel yelled and banged on the bedroom window, suddenly glancing sheepishly down at Avery, realising he had just sworn in front of an eleven-year-old.

She only stared up at him with those huge luminous eyes and smiled guiltily at the naughtiness.

He held a finger up for her to wait right there, bolted from the room, down the stairs and within moments was breathlessly back beside her holding the strange triangular box in one hand and banging on the glass of her bedroom window with the other.

"Reece!" Gabriel shouted. "Come back and get this!"

But down in the drive below Reece only laughed up at them, walking stiffly backwards with his arms outstretched in a lame imitation of a zombie and mouthing the words *I'll see you next Saturday!* before clambering onto his bike and peddling away.

Alone. Gabriel looked gravely back down at her. "You can never tell my . . . *our dad* . . . what we did."

She gazed up, nodding her head obediently.

He looked for a suitable place to hide it, hoping the girl would understand the seriousness of what he'd said.

Besides kiddie porn, the one other thing that was sure to have his father haemorrhaging with rage was 'dark magic' as Tia and his mother called it.

If he could he'd have banned Tia from the house with all her mystical ramblings. But she was his mother's best friend and his abilities to overrule his wife were limited. Besides, with her it was twinkly lights and frothy nonsense. Anything beyond the mad fantasies of the deluded were on a strict veto, whether that be supernatural books or possession horror films, even just the turn of the conversation towards anything of the occult or darkly sinister. 'Something from his younger years.' His mother had once explained when Oliver, ursine and bombastic, ridiculed, and chided Tia to such a degree it had left her in tears.

Gabriel opened the double doors to Avery's wardrobe, pushed the triangular box deep into the recess of the top shelf, put a blanket and a sweater in front of it and stood back to see if it could be seen.

It couldn't, but still the spot wasn't ideal. His mother was shopping for her in the morning and would, no doubt, be in there unpacking and hanging and positioning an array of things. He'd find somewhere else for it first thing then take it back over to Reece's.

Gabriel's face lit up. He'd forgotten about the twenty pound note his father had left for them.

"Come on, let's get a pizza." He said and led her towards the door.

He couldn't believe he'd forgotten. He was starving and pizza was his favourite.

Just like me. He self-castigated. *Head like a sieve you do boy.*

He glanced back at the wardrobe as he led her from the room.

Whatever you do idiot. Make sure you don't forget about that bastard thing!

The Uninvited Guest, the first day

The shadowy thing crept towards him, watching him in his sleep.

Gabriel stirred and rolled over. For a minute it thought the boy would open his eyes, but he only lifted a lazy leg to kick back the duvet, scratched his face and continued his dreams.

A hand reached down and touched his face.

He woke with alarm and saw her standing there, confused but unafraid.

"What's wrong?" he asked urgently.

She rubbed her groggy eyes.

"There's something in my closet."

"There," Gabriel said and then yawned. "No monsters."

He stood back and let Avery inspect the empty cavern of the wardrobe, her eyes moving slowly to each recess.

Eventually she smiled and wriggled back down in her bed.

"Okay now?" asked Gabriel.

She nodded and smiled, settled herself into a pose in bed so angelic and sweet she looked like something off the front of a Christmas card in his eyes.

"Go back to sleep." He said gently and left her to the night.

It was twenty minutes later when she woke him again.

"It's back."

Oliver, the first day

It was nice coming home with his wife in his arms.

He felt as he had in that long ago time, before marriage, before Gabriel, before . . . *before Avery.*

He'd been so proud to be seen with her when they first met. A woman so handsome, so determined, so strong. It was an honour that she'd picked him. She'd had no shortage of choices then.

The last few days of shock, betrayal and despair had left a shadowy dark crack running down the middle of their marriage. But curiously, had ended up being as effective as an intense course of couples' therapy.

They came home now to the quiet of their house, their feelings restored, renewed. Her arm around his waist, his over her shoulder.

They would do what they always did on nights like this. Go quickly to the bedroom and fuck quietly, muffle each other's moans and giggles, small quick noiseless movements lest Gabriel hear and come trotting in to see what was occurring.

He didn't want to break the moment, but something nagged within him. He thought of letting her go into the bedroom first and coming out with a quick excuse, *'I left my wallet in the car.' 'I think the kitchen lights are on.' 'I just want to check on Gabe.'* But she would see the guilt of a liar in his eyes, and he would break the painfully rebuilt trust between them.

There was only one way it could happen without ripping them back to the previous day's shreds and shards of tattered misery. Thankfully, she did it for him.

"Why don't you go check and see if she's ok?"

"I'm sure she's fine." He replied.

Please, insist woman, insist.

"Go on, you should."

"If you think I should. If you want me to."

Of course you don't fucking want me to.

"I'll wait for you." She smiled seductively and disappeared through their door, leaving him facing his daughter's bedroom.

His heart froze when he found her gone.

Internal arguments kicked off as he sat on her unmade bed.

Don't be ridiculous. She's just in the bathroom. The light is on in there, you can see it under the door.

But can you hear anything?

No.

Why would she be in there not making a sound?

It's been five minutes already.

Knock.

I can't.

Break the door down.

Don't be stupid.

Go and wake up Gabe.

As soon as he entered Gabriel's room the throat clenching terror of finding a child gone morphed into a flood of relief. She was there, safe, asleep, untouched.

Untouched?

The relief gave we to an unease that rose in him like a sickness.

Why in the name of God did he have her in bed with him?

He crept forward, fearful of waking either of them.

They were both dressed in bed clothes and laying back-to-back, an inch apart and sleeping in the comfort of each other's nearness like twins in a womb.

Maybe she'd been scared, woken in a strange huge house, not realising where she was for a minute, screaming. Gabriel would have come running.

Or suddenly swamped by the rolling wave of long overdue grief, finally hitting her less then two weeks after seeing her mother murdered on the kitchen floor in front of her.

Gabriel would have come running to her sobbing lament as well as her fear.

He would have rocked her. Stayed with her if she'd begged him too. Listened to her pain, her anguish.

Gabriel could be a good listener.

Gabriel could be many things.

He dipped his arms under the duvet and fished her out.

She melted into him as he carried her across his room. He glanced in the mirror to see his son stir and turn over, but thankfully not wake.

The conversation that needed to be had would be better suited to the unblinking light of day.

When Oliver finally slept, his dead brother Tad, tore his way through the underside of night to draw him from his dreams.

At least his sister Ellie had the decency to call first when invading his nightmares.

It was the Carsten house to which his brother bade him follow. Not the Carsten house of silk cushions and marble counters and granite tiles. The Carsten house of yesteryears. Huge and rambling. Sagging through the strain of its weight. Boarded shut, weathered, and beaten. Ripped of tiles and punched by the winds of the east. The Carsten house of his childhood. The crumbling Carsten house of ruin.

Where the Carsten triplets were born and grew to early adulthood.

Where two of them died before the age of twenty-three.

He followed his dead brother towards it, barefoot and shivering on the mossy ground. It stood atop a great hill, gazing down at his approach with the yellow eyes of a hungry tiger.

Tad gave him nothing but the hunch of his shoulders, the back of his wrecked head to gaze at, as he led him up creaking stairs, their footsteps slow as a world revolving.

He knew which room he'd draw him to. The attic bedroom, *of course*. The Carsten house's tangled mind, its broken backbone, its bleak beleaguered heart.

Ellie hung there still, roped to the beam by her bedsheet and swinging gently like a pegged robe on a washing line, swaying in a summer breeze.

Tad took his place below her, just where fate had left him, in his very last moment of life, the bullet that Ellie had fired from the Smith and Wesson Model 19 Revolver right through his brain still lodged in the blistered wooden floorboards three feet in front of them.

The pool of blood and brain matter glistened in fresh crimson, as if his long-ago murder had only happened moments before.

Tad propped himself on one brittle elbow, drew back one of Ellie's bony feet and sped up her swing, like an overgrown baby whose fingertips could just now reach the elusive mobile toy that had taunted him with twirling lights and magic. Taking great delight, he batted her back and forth. Oliver's dream-mind feared her broken neck may slip through the noose any second and she'd crash to the floor and break like glass.

'It's a family thing.' Tad croaked and pointed to the pool of blood in front of him, beckoning Oliver come forth and see what he could see, reflected there in its glassy red surface.

'He must get it from me.' Tad grinned, his smile lopsided, creaky, as though he hadn't used it in centuries.

Oliver stumbled forward and saw them together, an image of them, in the glassy pool of red blood, clear and succinct as if it was an image from a television screen. His son. His daughter. Laying together, an inch apart, back-to-back in the same plush bed.

Oliver wanted to stamp in the blood, like a child in a rain puddle, break the image into a thousand watery pieces.

But he could do nothing but stand in his imprisoned dream spot and observe what his brother wanted him to see, like some ethereal CEO conducting a ghost world presentation, laying out facts for Oliver's attention.

'He's a handsome boy.' Tad rasped with a broad lipless smile. *'Really, he must get it from me.'*

'There is nothing of my son in you!' The words screamed across Oliver's brain like a high-speed train.

And in this dream world not even his thoughts could be hidden. Tad answered him with venomous glee.

'Your son? By my reckoning I'd say that one belongs to me.'

Oliver's mouth filled with the taste of memory and sour milk.

Ellie's see-saw swinging suddenly ceased and she lifted her dangling useless head to look at him with eyes like two cuts that could never heal.

In her bony hand she held something; the Smith and Wesson Model 19 revolver, the same gun she'd used to murder their brother decades earlier. She offered it to Oliver with a gummy smile that said *'You need this now, it's a family thing.'*

Around them the room creaked and groaned, watching, waiting.

Oliver stared at his grinning brother. And his brother stared back with idiot indifference.

Vermin have a way of telling each other about these things.

Oliver tore his eyes from the offered gun, turned and fled the room, trampled down the stairs through the gluey wetness of the dream that held him, fought his way through the broken door of his fears and fled out into the night to try to find his way home under a sky as black as dread.

The Carsten House, the first day

Midnight.

Finally, all in the Carsten house were quiet.

Games were over and dreams were done.

All slept.

Except the uninvited guest.

There in the shadows with extraordinary stillness and a patience not of this world or the next, he waited.

And watched.

Chapter Four

Oliver, the second day

Every time the thought came up, he tried to push it back down, but it continuously resurfaced like a bobbing corpse.

Gabriel sat on the couch beside him in blissful ignorance.

His son was wearing one of the pink party hats cocked sideways on his head and lazily blowing up a succession of pink balloons. He seemed happier than he'd seen him in years.

Why?

Was it Avery's sudden introduction to the family? To his son's life?

The thought nagged at the back of his mind like an ancient debt.

If he raised it, he'd ruin the boy's mood for hours, perhaps days. And the 'Welcome Avery' party would be marred by the ugliness of it all. But try as he might, he couldn't let the thought go, it was sinking deeper into his mind like a parasite and spreading there with stubborn malignancy.

Gabriel was now watching him arranging a succession of pink cupcakes onto a circular stand, assuming the tension in his father's face was due to concentration of the task at hand.

Gabriel let go of one of the half-filled balloons and let it twirl and spit its way into Oliver's face.

Gabriel laughed heartily.

Oliver already hated himself as the words left his mouth after batting the deflating balloon away.

"Looked in on you last night."

Gabriel picked up a magazine and held it in front of him like a shield, finally answering, nonchalantly. "Oh yeah?"

"Not sure that was such a good idea, you letting her sleep with you like that."

Gabriel chose not to respond and the silence sat between them like the stench of rotting meat.

"What do you think?" Oliver finally asked.

"What do I think?" Gabriel answered, taking the magazine angrily away and revealing a face bruised with hurt and old memories. "I think it was the good idea of the century."

And there he goes, angrily up to storm off like a sulky teenager and relive the horrible time in his mind, let it play there on multiple repeat, ugly and obscene as a snuff film. Well done Carsten. This is going to be quite a party.

"Tell you what." Gabriel turned at the door to snap back at his father. "Next time we have a visit from one of your unknown offspring, you stay in and chase the monsters out of their closet, I'll go out and get pissed."

He pushed passed Tia who was just arriving, full of bright cheeriness and love for him, opening her arms, beckoning him in.

"Angel boy!" she called to his retreating back and watched him charge up the stairs.

Bemused, Tia turned to Oliver, angrily positioning the last of the cupcakes on the stand. She observed the décor of pink, covering almost every inch of the otherwise tastefully decorated room and mused that it looked like a unicorn had gorged on candyfloss then charged about throwing up in the place.

67

Looking at Oliver's face she decided her analogy may not be in the best taste and chose to ask instead. "So, where's the guest of honour?   "

Oliver got up, wiping angry hands covered in icing dust on his trousers. "You tell me. You're the psychic." He growled.

Avery, the second day

The horror that met Vivien Carsten when she flung open the double doors to Avery's bedroom closet blazed through her bones like wildfire.

Avery sat on the bed, watching her from behind, mindlessly combing the orange woollen hair of the ragdoll in her lap and making a half-hearted effort to keep the smirk from her face.

She skated her big blue eyes up and down the length of Vivien's body. It had turned stiff like a corpse with rigor mortis and her hands were clenching the handles of the closet doors so tight the bones in her fingers looked ready to snap.

Avery kept words to herself because that way she had power. That way she was strong.

Vivien, however, was not so formidable and without turning round to look at her, questioned with a voice so strangled with rising tension Avery imagined huge vessels in her neck bulging out like balls from chewed bubble-gum, pushing the limits of their tensile strength, stretching so far, they'd hopefully pop and cause her instant death.

"Avery," Vivien began, desperately trying to sound measured, controlled. "I bought three dresses for you this morning and hung them in your closet."

Vivien turned and stepped aside to allow Avery view of those dresses, now lying in a mishmash tangled jumble of white silk ribbons and lace on the closet base.

"They're now crumpled all over the wardrobe floor."

Excellent. Your powers of observation are top drawer old woman. You'll go far.

Vivien glared sternly down with an *'explain yourself young lady'* insistence in her eyes.

Truth be told, Avery had no idea how they'd gotten that way. Her best guess was the old cow had done it herself only to be able to run down to husband and son in full melodramatic victim mode, fling herself across the kitchen table. *'I'm trying so hard. I'm trying so hard.'*

Poor poor mama bear. Go get you some more botox and climb back in that bottle of gin.

Avery shrugged with grand indifference.

A little icing for your cake?

Vivien sighed, wearier than death, then bent down and picked up one of the dresses, smoothing out the crumples as best she could. "I think you should wear this one. I've never had to cater for a little girl before, but I was told these were all the rage."

Vivien hung the dress on the door of the wardrobe, bent down to Avery on the bed and began to unfasten one of the snaps on her old tatty pinafore dress.

Get back from me shaman!

Avery squirmed like an epileptic in the most violent of fits, causing Vivien to tumble to the carpet.

After an icy moment she clambered off the bed, gave Vivien her best *'you fucking-this-or-that'* look that could never be explained, never land her in trouble, stepped over her as though she was a dead fox buzzing with flies on the side of the street and sat calmly at her little dresser, took out crayons and her sketchpad and began drawing, her kitten-pink tongue poking out of her pressed lips in deep concentration.

Vivien's limbs went loose. Her head dropped with the weight of defeat. She prayed for strength in a body that now felt only made up of stitched cloth and stuffing, like Avery's treasured ragdoll who remained on the bed watching her with button blue eyes and a cruel grin.

Vivien used the bed and the wall to bring herself back onto unsteady feet.

"Wear what you want to the party Avery." She said in a frail voice that came close to tears. "But while you're in this house I ask that you treat me with just a little bit of respect. I think that's the least I'm entitled to, don't you?"

Avery only answered by letting her right leg swing; purposeful, direct, aimed with intent, and a surprising amount of power for such a slight eleven-year-old.

Up-down. Up-down. Up-down.

Kick, kick, kick.

With her every upward thrust her scuffed Mary-Janes came ever closer to the whiter than white paintwork of the Carsten house walls.

Up-down. Up-down. Up-down.

Kick, kick, kick.

Vivien's eyes followed with unbearable anxiety. As if she were watching her son play the winning game at a Wimbledon final.

Up-down. Screw-you. Up-down. Screw-you.

Kick, kick, kick.

Chip. Chip. Chip.

The Mary-Janes dug into the paintwork, leaving patterned marks of black rubber in their wake.

Vivien patted her chest and left the field of battle. Only pausing to glance down at the curious artwork Avery was creating in her sketchpad.

Her closet.

Doors flung open. Dresses crumpled and ruined on the floor. An ugly incarnation of a woman she had to assume to be herself, boo-hoo-hooing on the right. A strange triangular box set up on the top shelf and from within . . .

From within, the barest shape of a figure, peering out from the depths with a wide and staring disembodied yellow eye.

Gabriel, the second day

He'd decided to forgive his father.

Even if he hadn't, he wasn't the type to have let the injustice and his wounded feelings wreck anyone's special day.

His mother had gone to too much trouble and, besides, it was for her, for Avery, and he found he was loving her more with each passing moment, looking forward to waking up and being a little girl's big brother. Loving the way she looked at him, like he was her whole world entire. Loving having the feeling that Oliver had once explained to him, the feeling of what it was to be a father, a protector. *My whole reason for being on this earth is to look after you. Make sure you're happy. Make sure you're safe. God handed over that privilege from the first moment you came to me.*

And she had come to them.

To him.

I found you. I found you. I found you.

So thumped the beat of his heart.

Oliver had found him soon after the hellish conversation. He was in his bedroom trying to stave off angry tears.

I'm sorry boy.

His father had held him.

And when he went to break away his father drew him back, wanting to keep him longer sunk into his chest, as if to remind him he was his first born child and always would be.

He was the man who held his hand when they'd trampled through snow a decade earlier, then spent long minutes in front of a fire with him, rubbing his little feet with hands like blankets, getting the blood flowing from his heart back down to his toes again.

There are ways only a father knows how to rub your feet.

Gabriel would rub her feet for her.

One day.

For now, he sat on the couch between his mother and her best friend and awaited her arrival.

All around him little known relatives, hardly seen friends, chatted and gossiped and stuffed their silly faces with sugar and meat, never stopping to think what they were doing to their arteries or the fact that were consuming slices of what once had had a soul with mindless greedy indifference.

He knew why'd they come.

Murder always tempts the prying snooping curious. As does gossip. And they had the ultimate double-whammy artifact up in one of the spare bedrooms readying herself to be revealed, the bastard daughter of their acquaintance and sole survivor of the most egregious murder-suicide to have occurred in that area in years.

He glanced over at his mother's solemn face and wondered if her dour mood was also down to the hypocrisy of the party guests' readiness to cram themselves into their living room, waiting to feast on her like a quick easy meal.

"Young man I know just what you were doing in here last night when you had this place to yourself!"

Tia's words stole him from his thoughts, he looked at her in mild panic. He glanced guiltily at the marble fireplace. Where the triangular device had stood the night before, now sat a three-tiered cake under a banner screaming 'Welcome Avery.'

"You do?" he said meekly.

Tia nodded at a pretty young blond girl on the other side of the room who, unbeknown to Gabriel, was continuously flicking her eyes over to him.

"We've only had a few dates." He told Tia. "It wasn't her I had here last night. It was Reece."

"Well, that's a relief." Said Vivien sarcastically, finally lifting her mood enough to enter the conversation.

"Do you think . . . " Gabriel began sheepishly. "Do you think there's anything to worry about if you play with . . . "

His voice trailed way.

His mother and her friend homed in on him from either side, attention and suspicion now imprisoning him between them. There was no way out of this now. Only through. "Is it wrong to play with Ouija Boards?"

"Oh Gabe!" Vivien quickly glanced across the room at Oliver to make sure he hadn't heard.

"I wouldn't worry about those angel boy." Said Tia.

"Really?" said Gabriel with mild relief.

"Don't encourage him." said Vivien.

"Come on," said Tia "you think there's something inherently dangerous about something mass produced in a factory in China, slapped in cardboard and plastic and sold at Toys-R-Us for £18.99?"

"So you couldn't. . ." whispered Gabriel?

Tia cut him off abruptly. "Communicate with discarnate beings? Conjure up the forces of evil? No, Gabriel, you couldn't. Not unless they're suddenly selling them with a printed warning

'Playing with this toy may condemn your soul to a fiery lake of burning sulphur for all eternity'. They're parlour games, showmanship, entertainment. Any messages that do come through are only from the subconscious mind anyway."

Gabriel relaxed, convinced by her certainty.

She reached for one of the cupcakes from the swirling stand and took a large bite.

Through a mouthful of cake, she added. "It's only if you were ever to get your hands on a real one you'd have anything to worry about."

"A real one?" Gabriel suddenly felt every nerve in his body constrict.

"A rolling table or squdilatc board" said Tia "Any kind of authentic spirit or talking board. Any genuine divining device."

Vivien put a hand up to silence her friend. "Gabriel why are you so interested in this?"

Gabriel's eyes fell to his lap.

"The dead aren't always silent Gabriel." Said Tia. "And they aren't always still. They don't always rest easily in their graves."

Vivien shook her head at her friend, imploring her to stop. But Gabriel looked back from his lap to Tia, begging she go on.

"The human soul is a powerful thing. Sometimes when a person dies, suddenly and unexpectedly, their body dies, but the mind doesn't always die straight away." Tia said.

"They think they're still alive?" asked Gabriel.

Tia nodded. "And the immenseness of those emotions; love, passion, desire, doesn't dissipate, it can't be cut off so suddenly. It can only be converted into some other form of existence. It roams, as with the spiritual being, surviving bodily death, searching for its way home."

"And what if the emotion was a darker one?" Gabriel asked cautiously. "What if you hated me? Wanted to kill me? And suddenly died? If someone opened a doorway with one of those things – could you come back? Could you come back and try again?"

Tia the friend was gone. The woman who was blessed with an ear for the angels and cursed with the extrasensory perception of whatever else roams the world at night was here now, listening.

"Gabriel what have you done?" she asked coldly.

"Alright enough! Enough!" Vivien lifted her voice, this time not caring even if her husband did hear. She turned to Tia. "Elvira! You stick to palm reading and tea leaves." She turned to her son. "And Gabe, you keep her coffee house crap out of your head. Life's a rash, then there's death. And the itching's over." She bent close to her son. "There are no . . . "

Something stopped her mid-sentence. Something she was seeing over Gabriel's shoulder. Something which made her heart slow to a splashy beat.

" . . . ghosts." She finally said.

Gabriel turned to see what had pulled Vivien so bellicosely out of the moment.

It was Avery.

The pinafore dress was gone, as were the scuffed-up Mary Janes.

She'd relented and put on one of the dresses his mother had got for her that morning.

The moment seemed made just for her.

A six-year-old ballerina entering her first recital. Every eye in the room upon her, as protective as a soldier's, as adoring as a grandmother's.

Chatting, chewing, drinking stopped. Time seemed to stop in conjunction with the crowd's reaction.

The room gasped as one, but even that didn't drown out the gasp that came from Oliver.

Where have you been? My blue-eyed girl?

Where have you been? Darling one?

So thumped the beat of his heart.

All eyes moved with her as she crossed the room, the debutant, entering a world of ice pink magic and glitter. The little dress swishing like water and moving like a bell as she walked. Tiny polite footsteps across a room where the adoring eyes that watched her were only those of strangers and the tender gasps that shadowed her were of those who were not friends.

It was Vivien she went to.

The motherless girl, needing a mother.

The traumatised child, needing a friend.

She climbed into her lap, pushed back her long tumble of curls, and whispered in her ear.

Eleven words. Eleven words for Vivien. One word for each year of her short life thus far.

Words that were her anomaly. Words that were her due.

Vivien pulled back with the cold pallor of death on her face and stared down at the unsavoury little monster in her lap.

The air sat still and thickly between them like a warm rotten mist.

Avery smiled. A smile of sickly sweetness and everything that was ugly and wrong.

All around the party guests still cooed and marvelled at her beauty and the room vibrated in every shade of sugary pink.

But all that was reflected in Vivien's eyes was the ghost of a life she now could not believe or accept as a life that was her own.

Tia, the second day

By the time Tia was leaving a dull sunset was painting the whole sky pewter.

She'd been the first to arrive, to help with the setup of things. And now the last to leave, to tidy and clear and wash the opulent Carsten house surfaces clean of any spills and damage from the party that day. Such was the work of best friends. Best friends and the lonely who had no particular place to go and no significant other with whom to have no particular place to be.

But today Tia was keen to leave.

She loved the Carsten house and those in it and the sky above it.

Maybe it was just the way the rooftop pointed towards it but the sky above that house always seemed larger, more unreachable, than ever it did in any other corner of the world. A blanket of mystery, settled like an audience over a house while it waited for the ending of a story yet to unfold.

Everything about the house, and everything in it, always felt a little bit hers.

Vivien was hers, in the way a best friend always would be.

Gabriel wasn't her boy, her son, her child. But a tiny part of him belonged to her, as if the stars had ordained it.

"My son is your son." Vivien had often said to her, especially after a bottle of wine, no doubt guessing at what the pain of childlessness for a middle-aged woman must be.

As she sat in her convertible car, waiting for Vivien so she could leave, anxiety leapt and licked at her insides. It had started when the little girl climbed into her best friend's lap to whisper something in her ear.

A chill wind had seemed to whistle through the chambers of Vivien's heart at that moment, like the crying of a lost child, and, as is also the duty of best friends, Tia felt it accordingly.

She'd kept her distance from the child, not wanting to look at it, or talk to it, there was something in the girl's eyes she was certain she had no want or desire to see. So instead, she busied herself with her best friend duties. As soon as the last of the guests had left, she scrubbed and tidied, folded napkins, threw out rubbish, put away foldable chairs. But try as she might to create purity and order, *nothing*, nothing about the Carsten house that day, felt clean.

When Vivien came out of the house to join her at the car, party bag in hand, her eyes were still sunken and sad, like the burnt remnants of grief. They'd been that way ever since the girl had drawn back from her face.

Tia took the bag and tossed it straight inside her glove compartment, clicking the lid firmly shut, determined not to have to be reminded of anything about the party or this day.

"Haven't got room for an eleven-year-old in there have you?" Vivien asked with a heavy heart and Tia immediately wanted to pull her into the car with her and carry her far away.

Tia took her friend's hands in her own, turned them over and studied their palms, her eyes tracing the route of her lifeline.

Vivien knew what she doing? "Trying to see how it's all going to end?"

Avery laughed from behind them.

They looked over to see Gabriel spinning her in huge frantic circles on the merry-go-round.

Vivien lent on the car door, bent in closer to Tia, whispered. "I already know. It's going to end in tears."

Suddenly Oliver was with them, by contrast his mood was excitable and free, he was as dizzy with life as the wooden ride that carried his daughter round in endless circles. He straddled Vivien, muzzling his face into her neck and putting his hands face up on either side of hers for Tia's perusal. "Go on then Mystic Meg, what does it say in your crystal ball?"

Tia made effort to hide her strained mood, forced a smile for Oliver's benefit. "Oliver Carsten, how many more times? You're destined to become an award winning pianist reciting sell out nightly performances of Handel's Water Music at the Royal Albert . . . " her voice trailed away as she looked down at Oliver's hands, the forced jubilation slipping from her face like an ill-fitting mask. " . . . Hall."

Avery screamed again.

Gabriel was catching her round the waist and pulling her from the roundabout to spin her in circles in his arms.

Oblivious to Tia's cold mood, Oliver laid a firm strong kiss on Vivien's cheek and trotted off to join his son and daughter.

Alone again, Tia spoke frankly to her friend. "What was it she whispered in your ear Vivien? Tell me, what did she say?"

Vivien looked over at Avery. Gabriel and Oliver had her two feet in the air between them and, to her joyous delight, were swinging her like a hammock.

Vivien tried to speak but the words caught in her throat like glass. "She said . . . "

Tia nodded reassuringly, willing her friend on.

Vivien continued. "She said . . . she didn't give a cunting fuck what I am entitled to."

Tia's mistrusting eyes went back to Avery again. Now Oliver had her feet balanced on his own and was dancing with her in the grass. Gabriel laid on his back on the merry-go-round spinning in slow circles with casual indifference as he scrolled through his mobile phone.

Tia's voice turned uncharacteristically serious. "Tell Oliver he needs to be careful." She said.

"Don't tell me? He's no longer destined for the Royal Albert Hall?" said Vivien flatly.

Tia looked back at the girl for the last time, the sky above them rattled with the far off echoes of thunder and the promise of a storm which may, or may not, clear the sultry air.

"Those hands will bring him great fame." Said Tia, as if in a trance, and without further word for her friend turned on the engine of her car and tore from the drive, quicker than Vivien had ever, in a near lifetime together, known her to want to leave.

She turned to her . . . *family*.

They were together now, as one, a unit of three. All lying flat on the merry-go-round, heads lightly touching, feet trailing the mossy earth, staring up at an endless aching, storm brewing sky, as they turned slow circles beneath it.

She couldn't join them, their door was firmly shut to her, whether her husband or her son knew it or not. She was the scorned wife, the forgotten mother. The unwelcomed friend.

The uninvited guest.

It's a family thing.

The sky let her know it as thunder signalled its approaching nearness like the bang of a drum.

Vivien turned from them and went back to the house with the jagged scars of dread in her eyes.

Chapter Five

Gabriel, the third day

Gabriel sat at the desk in his bedroom in front of his computer and felt the demons of rage possess his soul.

"Jesus fuck!"

He bashed his fist on the desk, hysteria rising, a ferocious anger coursing through his system like venom from a snakebite. With every passing second, and every next click of the button on his mouse he felt the fury increase. He was aware of how he sounded, crippled with animosity, and festering with purulent surly-teen stink. But he neither cared nor tried to control it. She had invaded his most sacred of places, his two most treasured of possessions, his camera, and his computer.

Sure, she'd meant well, the slideshow he was indignantly clicking through had clearly been designed to touch him, to endear him to her even more than he already had become.

Avery in a sunhat with heart shaped glasses.

Avery superimposed in front of the Eiffel Tower in Paris waving him a big hello.

Avery next to the Statue of Liberty copying her pose.

Avery as a band member alongside the rest of the Spice Girls.

Avery on a rocket ship to the moon blowing him a kiss.

If he hadn't been so incensed by the utter invasion of his privacy, he'd have been blown away by her IT and photoshopping skills.

Not to mention her prowess for being able to crack the code to his password and steal into his inner world, as uninvited and unwelcomed as the devil itself.

Maybe this was all part of the new sibling experience. Reece had tried to explain it to him before.

They drive you so insane you literally want to rip off their heads and drink their blood. But woe betide anyone else do anything to even remotely upset them. Then you go to war.

He'd been an only child all his life. Never had to share. Not his parents love or a jellybean. He knew he was wrong for hating her for it. But the demons of rage that possessed him were winning. He stormed off his chair to find his parents, just before the slideshow ended and a message appeared for him:

To my big brother Gabriel. I hope you like it. Love Avery. x

Vivien, the third day.

Victory!

The little brat had fucked herself good and proper this time.

There'd be no way back from this. She'd once had the misfortune to nose through her son's laptop to find out if he was being bullied online in the middle of the bad year, as is the want of any mother, you can only ever be as happy as your saddest child's pain.

He found her spying . . . prying . . . and worked himself up into a wild rage that didn't subside for minutes. Followed by a sulk that didn't recede for hours and a period of isolation for her that he wouldn't relent and allow her back from for days.

Your turn now little miss. Let's see your world come crashing down around you, shall we?

Avery had pressed herself hard against her bedroom wall, shielding her face from the three of them, trying to burrow her whole body into the paintwork the way, days earlier, when Martin Black senior had attacked in a fit of deranged rage, she had tried to burrow herself into Gabriel's skin.

"I'm sorry! I'm sorry!" she shout-scream-bleated, the wall absorbing her words. They seeped out where they could from around her face in dull agonised lumbering bubbles of sound that arrived in the room like thudding footsteps.

Too bad bitchling, shoes on the other foot, damage is done. It's all gone to hell sweetums, you've had your day.

Vivien felt a slow hot grin ache to spread itself across her mouth.

She coughed it away and spoke in her most earnest of judicial *'mother knows best'* tones. "Gabriel's a very a private person Avery. He's very sensitive about people touching his things."

"I'm sorry! I'm sorry!" She yelled into the wall's thick density. Her mouth no more than a millimetre from it. "I just wanted to make him happy. I just wanted to give hm a gift."

"How the hell did you work out the password to my computer anyway?" Gabriel demanded.

That's it son. You tell her. Now pick her up and slit her throat and we'll all three bathe in the hot sweet blood of a virgin bastard bitchling.

Oliver sat on the bed like Switzerland, not sure who to admonish, who to comfort and who to agree with.

"His privacy is the very least he's entitled to Avery." Vivien went on. "I'm sure you care about that very much, don't you?" she smiled. "About what people in this house are entitled to?"

Ah the sweet taste of the virgin blood of a bitchling. Ah the taste of victory.

Avery began breathing hard, heavy, as though some invisible force were laying itself against her back and compressing her little lungs.

The contempt fell from Gabriel's face immediately and he took an urgent step towards her, eyes full of clemency.

Don't listen to her bullshit.

"Stop breathing like that Avery." Vivien insisted.

Oliver took his hands from his face, the turmoil of not knowing what to do was gone, being rapidly replaced by concern, by fear.

Don't buy her act. Stop pandering to that poisoned barb.

"Avery." Vivien said, the tension rising in her voice.

The girl's breathing laboured, more painful, more frantic, like she was about to give birth, push some monstrous creature out of her gullet.

"Avery. Stop breathing." said Vivien.

I will not let you win.

"Avery!"

Gabriel came towards her, full of concern and utter forgiveness. "It's ok. It doesn't matter. Avery it's fine, really."

For Christ's sake Gabriel.

Her winning hand was slipping further and further out of reach.

The breathing stopped suddenly as if she'd turned to ice, or stone.

They froze with her, and the room held its breath, waiting for the next move from whichever member of this family wanted to be the one to show their hand.

Avery coughed violently and slid down the wall, leaving behind a shocking arch of fresh blood, startling against the white walls like the erratic brushwork of a Jackson Pollock painting.

They instinctively darted forward as one to catch her, even Vivien, bewildered, dismayed.

Oliver was there first, catching her in his arms and flipping her over, his eyes searching frantically through the tragedy of that pale and listless face. A face now covered in blood that she'd brought up from her insides like vomit.

"Dad look at these." Gabriel pointed to marks on Avery's legs, small, raised rings, as though she'd been burned by someone leaving a coffee cup on her too long.

Oliver lifted the edge of her dress and found further, larger marks of more wild and erratic shapes, crawling up her thighs.

"Call an ambulance!" Oliver bellowed at Gabriel who nodded, sickly pale and sharing in her trauma, then bolted from the room to find his phone.

Chapter Six

Dr Faulkner, the fourth day

What was to be done about Avery Miller?

What was to be done about Avery?

What indeed?

The great and majestic Doctor Thomas Faulkner sat in front of them in his grand office, the many certificates on his maroon walls framing him behind his desk, emanating, as if from him, like a giant halo and set of angel wings.

And the ponderings in the great doctor's mind were; *what was to be done about Avery Miller? What was to be done about Avery?*

They were, truth be told, all pondering the very same thing. Albeit for different reasons, theories, levels of resentment and echelons of guilt.

Just as Gabriel was contemplating whether to throw a certain portentous little hat in to the ring and propose that his new eleven year old sister's brutal maladies could potentially be down to him and his best friend inviting Satan round last Saturday night and giving him full licence to use her tiny body as his own personal plaything, his father spoke, and the thought settled darkly back down in him like a reprimanded dog.

"Doctor Faulkner, forgive me, you're a medical man, I'm an architect." said Oliver trying to control the anger that laced each word. "There are things you know that I couldn't possibly understand, but please, three doctors and eight hours of tests and the most you can tell me is, there's nothing wrong?"

"Mr Carsten-" Dr Faulkner began.

Oliver was quick to cut him off. "I mean did you see her yourself? She was coughing up blood for Christ's sake. And what about those marks all over her skin. These things are not our imagination."

"Mr Carsten please." Dr Faulkner soothed him and Oliver settled back in his chair, his rising emotions calmed enough to allow the doctor to speak. "What we are all interested in is getting to the root cause of what is troubling Avery."

Dr Faulkner nodded at them as though he were a teacher waiting for them to concur their agreement on the point he'd just delivered.

The Carsten's all dutifully bobbed their heads back like a trio of obliging children.

"A dissociative personality disorder would be understood, if not expected, considering what she's been through." Faulkner said.

"There's something wrong with her body not her brain." Snapped Oliver.

Dr Faulkner leant forward on his desk, his body language indicating the Carstens should pay close attention. "The International Society for the Study of Trauma and Dissociation states that the prevalence is between one and three percent of the population developing some form of psychological anomaly after surviving incidents far less stressful than the one your daughter endured."

Oliver shook his head, he wanted answers in the form of a bottle of pills or an injection, not psychobabble hypothesis.

Dr Faulkner seemed to answer his thoughts. "It's a condition which carries no shame I can assure you. Simply another one of the body's natural neurological defences. Have you noticed any recent changes in Avery's behaviour?"

The Carstens stared silently back at the doctor, none volunteering an answer.

"Anything to suggest there may be one or more distinct personalities alternately controlling her nature?" Faulkner asked. "Memory impairment or erratic behaviour outside the parameters of a child's natural imaginative play?"

Gabriel stole a quick guilty glance at his mother. Vivien's eyes were roaming the walls like a teenager, bored of a lecture from a teacher over a misdemeanour she had no concerns about being in trouble for.

"I'm not putting her away." Oliver suddenly blurted out and Gabriel saw Vivien toss her eyes.

Dr Faulkner smiled kindly. "I'm sure it certainly wouldn't come to that. We all simply want to help Avery return to her true nature."

Vivien cleared her throat. Gabriel knew that meant she wanted to contribute to the conversation and something about it felt like the threat of war.

Oliver looked warily over at her.

"The problem, Dr Faulkner," Vivien said curtly. "with us trying to help poor Avery return to her true nature. Is that we have absolutely no idea what her true nature actually is."

Oliver's wary look changed to one of anger.

Dr Faulkner stood up, indicating they should do the same. "Then that is what we must find out."

Only Gabriel lingered by his chair as his parents headed to the door, as if itching to ask a question of his own.

Dr Faulkner picked up on Gabriel's inner need, as if also being able to read his mind. "Was there anything you wanted to ask young man?"

Oliver looked round at Gabriel. Gabriel felt his father's glare on his cheek like a blast of hot air.

"If there was..." Gabriel nervously began.

Dr Faulkner nodded for him to ignore his father's intimidating glare and continue with the question.

"If there was a possibility it might be something else." Said Gabriel "It would be important to talk about it, wouldn't it? I mean, for Avery's sake?"

Dr Faulkner smiled at the timid young man. "Most conditions, when broken down and understood, can be attributed to certain factors, if not physiological or neurological then psychological or emotional is always a strong possibility."

"What if it was something else?" said Gabriel.

"Son, are you talking about something on a metaphysical plane?" asked Faulkner.

Gabriel nervously nodded.

"For fuck sake." Gabriel heard his father mutter under his breath.

Dr Faulkner looked sharply at Oliver, unimpressed by the unforgiving way he treated his son.

"Young man," Faulkner said to Gabriel. "I've seen my share of death. And while I cannot transgress the boundaries of professional ethics by sharing with you my opinions on non-corporeal matters. I can say quite conclusively that the only form of 'evil' I've ever seen grip or possess the human soul is that of a human being."

"I just want to know what's wrong with her." Gabriel said sorrowfully.

Dr Faulkner opened the door for them. "As do we all! And I promise you young man, we're only a few short steps away from discovering what that is."

Oliver, the fourth day

Three years earlier, the day he hit his son, he made an internal promise never to let the boy feel fear, or pain, because of him or his demons again.

He'd made his share of promises in life, not all of which he'd managed to keep.

And he had his share of demons.

On a warm day in June decades earlier he'd promised to be faithful to Vivien Margot Entwistle, and the eternal reminder of that broken promise was now lying heavily sedated on the other side of a sheet of glass on the children's ward of the local hospital, being quietly observed by his oldest child.

The day he hit Gabriel still stung in his memory like a burn.

He'd come home and found the two of them together in the attic. Him and his idiot new friend. He'd guessed they were drinking, smoking, possibly doing a few light recreational drugs, that wouldn't be the end of the world. It wouldn't be the end of anything.

But what he saw . . . *what they were watching* . . . that was the end of everything.

His idiot friend went home and Gabriel had cried and begged them to believe that neither he, nor said friend, had had any idea what they'd be viewing when they put that particular disk in seconds before Oliver's head emerged through the hatch to the attic. Vivien believed him, immediately. She'd have believed him if he'd told her the Sunday tabloids were full of the unwritten works of Nietzsche.

Oliver tried to believe him. He wanted to believe. But he also knew a lie, told often enough, can someday become a truth. So he took him to the park with his wife believing father and son were headed off for a nice gentle stroll to bond and clear the air in the warmth of a summer day. But as soon as they got out of the car and walked through the wet stone passage that ran under the bridge by the canal Oliver held him up against one of the rough stony walls and growled in his face. He shook him, trying to disturb all the hidden chips of truth and lies and half-truths till they broke free and fell to the earth in front of them and could be scooped up and analysed. It was the first time he'd ever put his hands on his boy. It must have shocked him, frightened him, stirred up the crazy mix of adrenaline and fear that will make you scream out anything.

"Yeah that's right. I'm fucked up. I'm sick in the head." Gabriel had lamented. And following that he'd held him coldly with eyes of wounded betrayal and borderline hate, he'd let those unknowable eyes trail up and down the length of his father's body and followed up with. *"Wonder where I get it from?"*

He hadn't kicked him, punched him, headbutted him, he hadn't broken his arms, got him in a chokehold, smashed his head into the brick wall behind him. He hadn't done any of those things.

But he had slapped him.

He'd slapped him hard.

He'd hit his only son that day.

He was filled immediately with deep agonising regret. And crushingly, as soon as he'd done it, he believed him, a thousand percent, without doubt or hesitation. He knew, just as he knew he may never have his son's trust again, that there was no part of his child that was either monstrous or stained. *His son, his heart, his beautiful, beautiful boy.*

He did his best to remember that feeling now, as he approached him. He could see the reflection of his forlorn face in the large sheet of glass, solemnly watching Avery sleep. But the recent conversation in the Doctor's office and Gabriel's strange, loaded questions had left the acidic taste of bile in his mouth.

"What the hell was that all about?" Oliver tried, but failed, to say it without any aggression in his voice.

Gabriel immediately spun round to him, and with the guilt of a secret drinker hid something behind his back as though he'd been caught with a bottle of whisky.

The measures of control and reason were gone. Oliver manhandled his son easily, pulled what he was hiding behind his back out of his hands effortlessly, his mobile phone.

Oliver saw what Gabriel had been searching for on the small screen *Dabbling with the occult* and his face contorted with rage.

"What the fuck have you been doing in my house?"

"Nothing." Gabriel's voice was weak, his face turning pale. "Nothing."

Oliver leant towards him, even without touching him, he pushed him up against the glass. "Know what I'd do to you if I find out anything funny's going on in my house."

"Think I can guess." said Gabriel with small audacity.

Oliver thrust the phone back into Gabriel's belly where he caught it with both hands.

"Man dies the same way he's born Gabriel." Oliver told him fiercely. "Cold, alone, and screaming. After that there's nothing." He stood back. "Don't ever speak of this again."

Oliver turned and left his son alone, walking down the hospital corridor with the slow measured pace of a funeral director.

After he'd hit Gabriel that day, he'd been the one to cry, to beg, to plead for his forgiveness and his understanding. All of which sweet, sweet Gabriel gave and gave and gave.

Later that afternoon he'd fallen asleep on the couch and dreamt of his siblings. They'd both been there in the caverns of his subconscious, circling him like sharks and just as ready to eat him up in a frenzy, remind him of the monster of all fuck ups, the Grand Poobah of all mother fucking hideous wrongs.

When he'd woken, he'd woken screaming.

Gabriel was shaking him back to the world, crying, he'd never seen his father so disturbed.

'It's ok dad, I do forgive you.' He'd said through his tears. And Oliver had realised that in his sleep-babble he'd clearly been talking about the 'great mistake'. *'It was hitting me wasn't it daddy? Is that what's still upsetting you? Is that what you're calling the monster of all fuck ups, the big mistake?'.*

Oliver stared at him through the haziness of a world he was reluctantly returning to and then did something perhaps worse than what he'd done by slapping him that day.

'Yes, yes son. Hitting you. That was the monster of all fuck ups. That was my life's greatest mistake.'

Then Gabriel laid his head on his chest and soon he was sleeping, not knowing that his father had just lied to him through his teeth.

Hitting you? The great mistake? No son. It doesn't even come close I'm sorry to say.

Evan, the fourth day

The tell-tale signs of the bubonic plague were buboes, huge blood and pus filled swellings in the lymph nodes closest to the spot where the bacteria had entered the skin.

But other, more misinterpreted symptoms of such times and tragedies, were of germs of another kind having found their way into man's inner depths.

The flat nonpalpable lesions with changing colours and varying patterns which rose to the surface of the skin of the people of the Middle Ages, along with fluid filled blistering sores were often thought to be the screams of their entrapped souls. Dreadful messages of the innocent, begging for help or salvation, alerting the world around them to the fact that down deep, they'd been invaded, inhabited, taken over and used as a puppet by the devil of death and ruin.

Evan Peterson had always had a fascination with such things.

It was what had led him into nursing. His choices were limited. A poorly paid medical career or become a historian. A role in the NHS had been much easier to attain.

She was a beautiful child. Perfect. Currently sleeping like a china doll and seemingly flawless in every way. Flawless, until you lifted the cotton sheet that covered her and were met with the array of elevated epithelial lesions dotted over her chest, arms, and legs. A whole network of seborrheic keratosis of verrucous, velvety, waxy, scaling and crusted surfaces were set upon her otherwise pure and untouched skin.

"Have you seen this?" Evan asked the night sister, picking up Avery's chart and studying it in the dim yellow light.

"Avery Miller-Carsten." Replied the nurse. "Eleven."

Evan wanted to know a lot more than her age and name.

He turned on the light of his pen-torch and moved in, examining the carbuncles with determined concentration like a mechanic, searching the mechanisms under the bonnet of a car to find out what was preventing it from running. "Jesus." He muttered.

Avery stirred slightly, her face contorting, as if to the sound of his voice, or the word he'd chosen to say, despite her drug induced sleep.

The night nurse felt her pulse. "They can't work out what it is. They're running more tests before she goes home in the morning."

"She's going home in the morning?"

"Her stepmother is coming to get her at 10.00 a.m."

The night nurse turned away and began replacing the bag of water on Avery's drip. When she looked back, Evan had put down his torch, picked up his mobile phone and was taking a succession of pictures of the marks coating Avery's body.

"What are you doing?" She asked urgently, her voice going from a raised tone to the hush of a whisper within the same sentence, glancing down at the girl to make sure she hadn't woken her.

Evan looked warily from the defilements invading the little girl's body to their images on his phone and then to the night sister. "I know what this is."

Chapter Seven

Evan, the fifth day

There was thunder in the air. This was going to be a bad one.

Oliver Carsten was already agitated. He'd wanted to pick Avery up from the hospital himself but had to finish the redesign of a vitrolite wall veneer for one of their top tier clients who were coming in for a progress report at the end of the day. The sudden addition to the family and all the various issues that had arrived with her had already put his erstwhile obsessively planned routine wildly out of whack.

There was a strange unease about the thought of the two of them alone together. But what else could he do? He had wanted to ask Gabriel to chaperone, but the boy was still sulking, moody with him. That or, in his presence his son now just felt . . . fear.

That wasn't what he wanted.

All he wanted was a return to normalcy.

The same number, that of an unknown caller, had already tried him seven times that morning and he could see a stranger waiting on the pavement outside the studio, his eyes clearly searching to pick Oliver's car out of the line of oncoming traffic.

Fucking press.

Irritation moved in him like worms under the skin.

If the man even tried so much as talking to him, he'd punch him into next week.

Oliver Carsten, those hands of yours will get you in trouble one day. You won't hit him. You'll politely ask him to be on his way.

"I don't talk to the press." Oliver snapped at the young man before he even had a chance to open his mouth.

Evan Peterson shook his head, perplexed. "Mr Carsten please."

"I DON'T talk to the press." Oliver bellowed.

"Neither do I!" Evan spat back and held his mobile phone, bearing pictures of Avery's blistered skin, in Oliver's face.

Ten minutes on they were in a café together, Oliver morosely stirring a cup of black coffee and waiting to hear what he had to say.

Evan composed himself, struggled his way out of his jacket, bent into Oliver's space and kept his voice low so others around them couldn't hear.

"Mr Carsten are you aware of what a factitious disorder is? Or the term 'malingering'?" Evan asked.

Oliver looked blankly at him.

"Have you ever heard of Munchausen Syndrome or Munchausen by proxy?" Evan continued.

"When someone wants to kill themselves?" Oliver replied, not sure if he was right.

"Not exactly." Evan put his phone down on the table between them. "Until recently such disorders were written off, laughed at. It's only with new understanding they've become an important factor in the diagnosis of certain cases."

He tapped into the photo-gallery on his phone and began scrolling through pictures as he spoke.

"Three years ago, I was treating a fifty-year-old man in Yorkshire. He was vomiting blood and his body was swelling, he was erupting in legions and welts. It was only through the medical staff's constant probing they realised he'd been slowly poisoning himself with a cocktail of cleaning products and store-bought medication."

Oliver looked at him suspiciously. "Why?"

"Diagnosis is often difficult as there is considerable co-morbidity with other mental disorders. However, our basic understanding is that a patient becomes addicted to hospital procedures or craves the attention and sympathy ill health brings." He glanced around the café, double checking no one was listening, leant in closer still. "When the condition is by proxy the person will poison or exaggerate conditions in a close relative, usually an offspring, for the same attention and sympathy."

"What's your point?"

"The youngest recorded diagnosed case of Munchausen Syndrome was a twenty-one-year-old. There has never been an incident where a child has been involved."

"Unless they were the victim?"

"By proxy."

Oliver picked up the phone, examined the pictures more closely.

"These are the exact same marks we witnessed on the skin of the fifty-year-old in Yorkshire." Said Evan.

"These are the actual pictures?"

"No Mr Carsten, this is your daughter. I took them in her room this morning before your wife collected her."

Oliver looked warily at the photographs again.

"She's either the youngest sufferer of Munchausen Syndrome I ever thought I'd come into contact with and is poisoning herself."

102

Oliver looked up at him.

"Or someone in your house is."

Vivien, the fifth day

"I've put your medicine in with your milk, so you won't taste it." said Vivien and crossed her leg in her atypical fashion, so her right foot rested on her left knee, manly and erotic just like Oliver liked it. She didn't fart this time. Instead, she buried herself in her laptop lest she have to engage in any further interaction with it.

It was sitting on one of the barstools opposite her, fervently drawing with crayons into her sketchpad.

She was remarkably calm, considering her recent traumatic spell in hospital. As calm as she'd been following seeing her own mother butchered right in front of her.

How could any child not crumble and break through the horror of that? Did the little beast have the devil pulling her strings?

Vivien didn't care what it was drawing. But wanted it to drink its milk and looked up to see if it was going to respond in any way to what she'd said.

It was deep in concentration at her sketching, little kitten-pink tongue poking ever so slightly out through those pursed lips again.

Vivien was about to repeat her comment, let her know she'd found a way to get that medicine down her more efficiently, get it pumped in and circumnavigating its little system, working its way through the alimentary canal, pumping with its blood through arteries, working its way through veins, circling its way through the twist of its capillaries, channelling its way to its brain.

"Avery." It didn't look up despite Vivien saying its name. "I said I've put your medicine into your milk so you can't taste it."

After an aching minute it glanced up from its sketching to the dosed-up glass o' milky-moo-drug-milk sitting on the kitchen island in front of her. "Aren't you clever." It finally said.

How could you hide from a murderer who lives under your skin?

We'd all be scared if we knew what was swept under the carpet of each other's imaginings.

"Drink your milk." Vivien sternly said.

Kick, kick, kick.

Up-down, up-down, up-down.

The little leg began swinging and a-kicking.

Swing, swing, swing.

Kick, kick, kick.

Those irritating feet of its were in converse boots now. It'd seemingly forgotten about the ugly-as-fuck Mary-Janes. On every upward kick, with a surprising amount of force for such a slight eleven-year-old, it came dangerously close to making contact with the edge of a high end £4,000 designer made granite kitchen island.

Vivien didn't care too much. Granite was strong enough to withstand such things. But one of her favourite pictures of Gabriel was set in a bowed silver Tiffany's frame and sat dangerously close to the edge. One of its kicks, if contact was hard enough, would likely knock it from its precarious position and send it on its merry way, destroying what she had loved more than life, all her life, smash it up to a thousand pieces on the opulent tiles beneath.

A high end £109.99 Damascus Chef's Kitchen knife with a double-edged blade, sat inches away from her hand and her mind itched madly in the darkness of her fantasies to thrust it into that tiny kneecap, severe ligaments and cartilage, make short work of tissues and tendon, hobble its ability to ever swing that loathsome leg again. Then wipe off its blood on the back of her jeans and stand over her saying '*try kicking now you grey sprinkle on a rainbow cupcake*' while on the floor below her the little bitch howled and wretched and screamed.

Vivien's blood ran slow and thick.

A message had popped up on the laptop of in front of her:

Dinner in the usual place this week darling?

Then folded itself electronically in two and sent itself into '*Oliver's personal file*' with immediate haste.

ACCESS DENIED

She tried the usual password, once, twice, three times.

GABRIEL-MARK

GABRIEL-MARK

GABRIEL-MARK

She sighed.

Access denied . ... denied . . . denied.

Don't go looking too deeply for the meaning of things.

GABRIEL MARK

MARK – GABRIEL

GABE MARK

GABE GABE GABE

Bitch be on your way.

Up-down, up-down, up-down.

Kick, kick, kick.

Fuck, she had to try it.

AVERY

Avery, how sweet.

Access denied.

Ok, good, good.

The converse boots made contact. Gabriel's picture jumped a little, with every upward kick it wobbled and jumped a millimetre closer to the sheer drop down the side of a granite island in the middle of an Aegean blue and white marbled tiled sea.

"Avery."

Kick, kick, kick. It ignored her.

"Avery."

Kick, kick, kick. She said its name again.

"Avery, what's your middle name?"

She kept sketching with grand indifference.

Finally, she let it be known. "Maye."

AVERY-MAY Vivien typed in with shaking fingers.

Access denied.

AVERY MAY

"With an 'E'" it said with the nonchalant confidence of a thoroughbred virago.

Her hands shook even more violently:

AVERY MAYE

"Oliver," she gasped, her hand flying up to her throat.

There was a picture of him with a woman. They were on a park bench together, enjoying each other in the warm summer sun. She, smiling wildly, wearing a £1,150 Stella McCartney dress, Vivien knew because she wanted it, she'd seen it in a magazine, and a red soled pair of a Jimmy Choos with a small little Jack Russell terrier sitting patiently by her heels.

She had an *'I'm going to take you for a walk soon'* hand motion for the dog and an *'I'm going to fuck another woman's husband tonight'* smile on her face. She was beautiful, like a model, like something out of the highest priced of magazines. And she was muzzling her adulterous mouth into her husband's neck for everyone in the park that day to see.

Kick, kick, kick.

Smash!

The converse boot made contact again and the framed photograph of Gabriel plunged in a suicide drop to shatter to a thousand pieces.

"Drink your milk!!!!!!" Vivien screamed.

Oliver, the fifth day

He raced back home to a scene as bleak as murder.

His mind had overset like a mighty cup of marbles, spilling in every direction, since he'd spoken to Evan Peterson earlier that hour.

He'd gotten back home in half the time it would usually take, and yet as he went through the door to the back of the house his whole world slowed with awful stop motion stillness.

When he'd reached the kitchen he found the two of them together.

The woman he once thought of as his wife had her by the throat. She was screaming at his daughter the words 'Drink it!' and trying to force a glowing glass of winter white milk down her struggling throat.

'I don't want it!' his daughter had been protesting and finally wound a tiny hand round a munificent fistful of her curls and yanked with all her might, shrieking 'Get away from me you stupid bitch!'.

The thing he had thought of as his wife all these years leant back and savagely slapped her innocent cheek.

It was then that he attacked. He barged into her like a rugby player and the match was on; tackling, scrummaging, evading, fainting, turning, twisting, mauling, rucking.

In the midst of their crazy dance he spotted the high end £109.99 Damascus Chef's Kitchen knife with a double edged blade up on the kitchen island and for a second thought of grabbing it.

His mind ran everywhere like ants in the dark.

Finally, his hands flew up like startled birds taking flight and clamped around her neck, where they squeezed and squeezed and squeezed. With the fury of a roman general, he squeezed.

The world crashed and shivered. When he was seconds away from killing her his mind yanked him savagely back to reality.

She slid down the kitchen cabinets, gasping, gagging, dragging in raw agonising air like a trout on sun bleached cobbles, begging for oxygen in the choking world.

He swallowed hard and stared around the kitchen, almost hypnotised. He felt suddenly alone in a stranger's house, in a cold and godless world.

Maybe we all have a wild and secret self somewhere.

Then his eyes saw her, and his being calmed, his murderous rage stilled. She was curled up into a frightened ball in the kitchen corner, as if trying to reclaim the foetal position, one terrified eye peering out through a creamy tangle of blonde, beseeching him for help.

I found you, I found you, I found you.

So thumped the beat of his heart.

No one's ever going to hurt you again.

Oliver Carsten was a man of many broken promises. A man of many unconquerable demons.

No one's ever going to hurt you again.

That was one promise he would never break. Never break again.

He rushed to the child and scooped her up, cradled her small shaking form against his chest, carried her out of the room and away from the thing on the ground that once had been his wife.

Husband and Wife, the fifth day

It was seven hours before they spoke.

They went back to the field of the battle. The place that had once been the family kitchen. The heart of any house.

It was now cold and heartless, filled only with electric blue stillness, even the dust felt weighted with lead.

They each knew there was no life for them here now, no chance for the marriage, nothing within the walls other than the slow death of days.

He spoke first. Though he couldn't look at her. His eyes burrowed into the granite island counter ten inches from where she sat. "Who are you?" he said in a low flat voice.

Vivien responded with nothing but her own loaded silence.

"You're very dangerous and very ill." Oliver said and finally investigated his wife's stony face.

"We all have our diseases." She said.

Oliver got up and went to the kitchen telephone, began to press numbers on the pad.

"Are you calling the police?" she asked calmly.

Oliver gave her nothing but his back as an answer.

"How would you like me to explain this to Gabriel?"

He turned to her. She had flicked her tumble of curls back and revealed the extent of the bruising his hands had left around her throat.

"Another one of your slips may be enough to finish him? Can you stand to murder your son?"

A third voice entered the room, muffled and indistinct, coming from the phone receiver in Oliver's hand. "Operator . . . operator . . . what's the nature of your emergency?"

Oliver slowly put the phone back on the pad.

"Leave this house tonight." he said. "Go to Tia's, go to your brother's. Don't ever contact me again."

They stared at each with the sternness of waring world leaders. Finally, Vivien got up. She took slow calm steps across the tiles, her heels clicking on the marble with the sound of castanets.

She stopped at the kitchen door, turned back to him before leaving the kitchen to go upstairs and pack a suitcase.

"They both still laugh at you, you know?"

"Tia and your brother?" Oliver asked indignantly.

"The Devil" said Vivien "and God."

Chapter Eight

Oliver, the sixth day

"I'm coming Avery!" he called through the night, and fought his way out of the sheets and blankets, staggering off the bed and charging in the direction of her screams.

She was sitting up in her bed, befuddled and disbelieving. A piteous sight, looking aghast at the fresh blood she had coughed into her hands and then up at him for her own salvation.

Oh Sweet Jesus, not again, not again.

"Daddy," she whimpered, her voice begging him to take the hell away.

And it was the worst sound he'd ever known. How could he help a child coming apart at the seams.

He pulled back her blanket and found her legs gone.

They both looked down at the bloody festering stumps, eyes wide with horror and disbelief. Then to each other for help, explanation, an answer to the insanity.

More blood then, gushing from her mouth as if from an overturned bucket.

Daddy, she was trying to say again, but all that emerged from her ruined throat was an incoherent bubbling bally squeal.

Her face collapsed, drawn and contorted. She fell into him. The stench from the rotting stumps of her legs filled the air like wet long gone off vegetables. She let out a low moaning cry, reached up to touch his face with a trembling tiny finger, then the whole of her infrastructure shattered, and she dissolved into herself, leaving nothing in her father's arms but a hundred pieces of her, burnt brown and brittle, like a flurry of autumnal leaves.

"Daddy."

Fuck!

Oliver woke with a sudden sweaty start and found himself on the chair in Avery's bedroom, sitting slumped beside her, in near enough the same position he'd been in when he fell asleep in her room an hour earlier, after watching from her bedroom window, as his wife got in a taxi and left.

He looked around the pale pink light of the room, as if needing to be further convinced it had only been a dream.

"Daddy." She was saying again. "There's someone in my closet."

"There's no one in your closet sweetheart." He said as kindly as he could.

"There is." She said nervously and slid further down in the bed, pulling the blanket up over her mouth and drawing her ragdoll in for safety.

He smiled. A smile that said '*I'll check it for you. Daddy's here. I'll chase all the monsters away.*'

And he went to the closet and opened the doors and within the merest of seconds the rotting corpse of Martin Black Junior was upon him, kitchen knife in hand, plunging it deep into the belly of his heart.

Avery screamed and pulled the blanket over her head.

Black pushed her father on to the bed on top of her, drew the knife out and forced it into her father's heart again and again and again.

"Dad."

Oh my fucking Christ!

Oliver woke in his own bed, his own room, and found them standing there in their nightclothes. His children, his two children, his son and his daughter. Standing in the dappled moonlight of his shadowy room having woken him from a nightmare within a nightmare within a dream of a dream.

This time he needed more convincing.

He sat up in bed and turned on the light. Looked around the room, looked at his watch, 2.15 a.m. Looked back at his kids. Ok, this was real.

It was real. But it was wrong. There was something in their faces, Gabriel's especially.

"Dad." Gabriel said again. "There's something we need to tell you."

Gabriel, the sixth day

His father had promised he would never hit him, never hurt him again. Three years ago, in a park on a Friday, he had promised him that.

Three years ago, he had lied.

Avery burst into tears immediately, crushing her doll into her chest, a mother must protect her babies from the wickedness of the world. From the things no child should ever see.

Gabriel had decided to tell him about the Ouija board, chosen to tell him, wanted to tell him. The guilt was overwhelming him. Even if they'd hidden it, taken it from the house, crushed it, buried it, posted it to China, he still couldn't be sure anything *unwelcomed* that their interference in such forces may have let into the house would leave.

He knew he had to enlist his father's help, whatever that may mean for him.

For some reason, some event, buried deeply in Oliver Carsten's history, had left him with an understanding of these things. Yes, he had contempt, intolerance, scorn, disdain for anything in the realms of the occult, but that would have come from some form of experience.

If they now had to exorcize a malingering being from their home, only Oliver would know what the process for doing so would be.

The sight of the triangular box and the guilt in his son's eyes was enough to explain what they had been up to.

Gabriel had thought of blaming the whole thing on Reece, explain that he'd brought it into the house and half tricked, half manipulated them into playing with it. But three years ago he'd

116

had to use Reece and his *'act now think later'* mentality to convince his parents that their only son wasn't turning into some woefully wrong and despicably dreadful shape of a man, a deviate monstrous beast.

Oliver sighed and looked at the box for a frighteningly long moment after Gabriel unwrapped it from the blanket and set it down on the coffee table.

The ticking of the clock on the wall beside them was the only sound in the room and the noise of it was crushing in on Gabriel's eardrums, evoking the memory of the night, six days earlier, when Avery had asked;

'How many nights before someone dies in this house?'

and it had answered;

Tick tick tick tick tick tick tick.

Oliver crossed the room towards him, holding him with his eyes, eyes that gripped him like steel.

Eyes that, if he'd been able to read them, would be clearly saying to his son *'You call the devil and the devil comes a-calling.'*

Tick tick tick tick tick tick tick.

He felt his legs go weak.

Three years ago, he had slapped him. He had slapped him so hard it left a yellow-purple lump under his eye that had to be explained to his mother as the result of his attempt to perform a *Frontside Half Cab Heelflip*, on the skateboard he never wanted, just to impress his father, despite having the most rudimentary and mediocre of freestyling capabilities.

But his mother had left the house that night and whatever Oliver decided the punishment for his son would be would require neither justification nor explanation. Not for Vivien at least.

117

When he reached his boy, he hit him. Not a slap, this time it was a punch, childhood games were over. This was a man, landing a mighty blow, into another man's face.

Avery's immediate flurry of tears reawakened Oliver to his senses. But he neither apologised nor bent down to Gabriel reeling on the couch to see if he was ok.

It would be minutes before Gabriel would recover. Only the persistent sobbing shrieks of his sister, refusing to leave him, despite their father ordering her to her room, brought him back to reality.

He watched Oliver give up his battle with her, throw his hands up in exasperation at her defiance, and leave the room.

Avery flung herself around her brother's neck, weeping bitterly.

Gabriel watched him through the living room doorway, traipsing back up the stairs with heavy footsteps that sounded like sombre military funeral drumbeats.

He watched him and wondered if the man in the house would ever, *could ever*, hold his hand on a long walk, through snowy winter, rub his feet in front of a fire, be a father in his eyes again.

Gabriel glanced through his watery vision and the swarm of spots that still danced across his brain, back to the triangular box on the table.

Hell is for half bred harmless monsters. All the demons of the universe live right here on this very street.

Ellie and Tad, the sixth day

Oliver climbed into bed in the early hours of that morning and did all he could to resist the urge to sleep.

He knew his brother and sister walked there and waited, waited for him in the darkest caverns of his dreams.

His mind fell back to the day of it. The memory of the Grand Poobah of all monstrous fuck ups, the hour of the 'great mistake'.

Their parents had obsessed over Ellie and her need to constantly wear black, panicked over her choice of the people she associated with, her habits, the moods, the tattoos, the heavy eye makeup, the black lipstick, the devil worship books she left around the house as if she wanted them to be seen.

The sweet little Ellie of yesteryears was gone and some self-styled jobless, aimless, zombie of intentional ugliness, grim clothes and dark secrets walked around in her place.

'She's not harvesting the blood of dead babies.' Tad had told them with grand indifference, and resisted their demands to be part of the intervention they'd planned for when she got back that day, instead he slumped in a chair in the corner of the living room and mindlessly picked up a magazine.

She didn't get back till two a.m. the next morning. Draped in black and doped up on God knew what, eyes spinning like whirlpools and skin so white it looked like it had been bleached.

The inquisition soon began.

'Where have you been?'
'With friends.'
'Which friends?'
'You don't know them.'

'We wouldn't want to know them.'

'Oliver help, help me please.' She said with only her eyes, as she searched beyond her parents' deliberate shoulders to find him.

Are you taking drugs?

Tad let a small laugh out from behind the magazine. 'No, she's harvesting the blood of dead babies.'

'Either help or go to your room.'

'Go to my room? Is that a joke? I'm nearly twenty-three.'

'Are you doing this to punish us Ellie?'

'Do you hate us?'

'Haven't we given you everything?'

'I can't take it any more Oliver' she said with her eyes.

'Are you ill?'

'Are you '*ill in your head*' she means.'

'Oliver, tell them, let's tell them now. Tell them what's been happening all these years.'

'Why are you leaving Tad?'

'I thought you wanted me to go to my room *daddy*.'

'Don't get smart.'

'I'm going to the attic.'

'To smoke a joint no doubt.'

'Yeah, to smoke a joint, is that alright? At least one of us should be honest about what we do behind closed doors around here.'

"You fucking hypocrite!" This time she wasn't saying anything with her eyes. This time she was screaming it, raging it, shrieking out loud enough to wake the devil himself. Then she turned back to Oliver and screamed something else.

"Tell them Oliver! Tell them what you've seen! Tell them what you know all these years that arsehole's been doing to me!!"

The seconds that crawled by before he answered her had felt like the endless stretch of eternity.

'Ellie you must be mad. That's our brother Tad. He's our brother. Your brother. What a wicked lie. I've never seen anything.'

120

And there it was. The great mistake. The monstrous fuck up of all hideous impossible, wrongness of wrongs.

The lie that set in motion everything that came next and left scars across his soul that would never ever heal.

If the twenty-two-year-old Oliver Carsten had been a man that day he would have said, *should have said*, 'She's right. There's something very wrong about him. Get off your pigging high horses mum and dad and call the fucking police.'

And it felt an equally desperate eternity before she in return responded to his lie.

She turned to him with sad dead eyes, ringed by black mascara laden tears. She looked at him as though she'd just been raped by another brother, the one she had trusted the most, the one she had thought would one day rescue her from the life of hell she'd been living in.

"You call the devil." She said without smiling. "The devil comes a-calling."

So as her beloved brother Oliver chose not to end the suffering for her, she, instead, ended it herself, by putting a bullet from her father's Smith and Wesson Model 19 revolver through her other brother's brain, up in the attic while he toted on a joint, and subsequently bought her own ticket to join him in hell, courtesy of the bed sheet she tied around her neck from the overhanging beam.

They had got through the door just in time to see it. The gunshot clashing through the house like thunder had brought them running. So yep, the final *'fuck you'* for mum and dad and poor, poor Oliver, was to get there just in time to see Ellie snap and swing, having reduced the Carsten triplets down to one from their erstwhile three.

121

She'd had time to write a note, addressed it to Oliver. His father found it and refused to let him see it. But Oliver demanded.

Dear Oliver

Thank you.
Now I know why Satan is the only man I could ever trust to do right by me. You wouldn't understand. It's a family thing.

Ellie

Oliver turned over in bed, eyes wide and empty, staring at the insignificant wall.

He was strong enough to resist sleep and the demons that lurked therein.

He was strong enough for many things.

Gabriel may have been sufficiently stupid to open a door that he didn't have the strength to close.

But Oliver did.

Oliver Carsten was strong enough for many things.

He checked his phone. 4.46 a.m. He would lay here another hour without sleeping then get up, douse that thing in petrol, stick it in a barrel in the garage and set it ablaze till it burnt to a crisp, send it back to the hell from which it came.

Chapter Nine

Gabriel, the last day

"What happened to your eye?" Reece was saying from within in the small square window in the right upper corner of Gabriel's computer screen.

"Fell down the stairs, didn't I?" answered Gabriel solemnly.

He'd been in his room for twenty minutes, performing the mindless task of deleting the three hundred plus pictures they'd taken to throw light in his path when he needed to find his way into the attic and return the Carsten house to light, exactly one week ago today. If only he'd known then that it would be the exact opposite of *light* he'd be letting into his home that night.

Reece's picture had popped up several times, insisting they talk. He'd ignored him at first. The mindless task of deleting endless pictures of black nothingness was helping to keep him distracted from his thoughts, but only for so long. Soon those thoughts turned to his father and the pain he'd caused him. And not the pain that his friend Reece could clearly make out via the bruise on his face, despite his image only being remotely broadcast to him through the wonders of wireless technology.

Reece's father was a loveable fool. Reckless, childlike, pretty unsuccessful in life, and harmless as a butterfly. Reece had never known fear. It was only when he was around Oliver Carsten when he was in a certain mood, he felt the sickly presence of unease.

There were things he wanted to say to Gabriel, but male bravado prevented it. He needed to change the subject and find a segway out of talk that might transgress to the ugly vagaries of human nature.

"I need to come over and pick up that thing." Reece said.

"What thing?" asked Gabriel.

"You know, that box I left at your house last week."

"Sorry blud, that's toast."

"What?"

"The old man cremated it this morning."

"Gabe, what?"

"You know what he's like."

Without intending to Reece made a direct nod to Gabriel's bruised eye and loaded his voice with sarcasm. "Clearly." he quickly covered his tracks. "Seriously bro, I need to come and get it."

"Reece, I'm not joking. He burnt it when he found out what we did."

"Gabriel. It was a metronome."

"What?"

"A metronome. An antique one. My brother uses it when he practises guitar, he's currently looking all over the house for it and threatening to kick my arse up and down the street."

Gabriel let out a small incredulous laugh. "Reece, for the past week I've been thinking my new little sister's been housing Old Nick rent free."

"Man, I was fucking with you! I wrote the YES and NO on it with a magic marker."

"A magic marker."

"Yes."

"A magic marker."

"You know, a fucking felt pen."

The boys sat at their respective computers, so tense their images seemed frozen as if the network connection had suddenly failed.

Finally, Reece moved and spoke. "I can't believe he burnt it."

"I can't believe you exist!" Gabriel snapped and angrily reached with his mouse and ended the call. It was nowhere near as dramatic as the days of old when one could slam down a phone receiver, nor as cathartic.

Gabriel's inflamed anger festered as he returned to the menial job.

Pictures of nothing. Pictures of nothing. Pictures of nothing.

Delete. Delete. Delete.

Pictures of nothing. Pictures of nothing. Pictures of nothing.

Fucking Reece.

Delete. Delete. Delete.

Pictures of nothing. Pictures of nothing. Pictures of nothing.

So what was all the shit about a man in her closet?

Pictures of nothing. Pictures of nothing. Pictures of nothing.

Delete. Delete. Delete.

I hate my dad.

Delete. Delete.

All this over nothing.

Delete. Delete.

Pictures of nothing. Pictures of nothing. Pictures of nothing. Pictures of nothing. Pictures of nothing. Pictures of nothing.

He froze and his heart froze with him, stubborn disbelief soon giving way to a drowsy terror which stole into his veins.

Within a set of three hundred pictures of black empty nothingness was suddenly something. There in the hatch that led up into the attic, blurred and indistinct, but undisputable, undeniable, irrefutable, real.

A man's face.

The Thing that Waits in the Closet, the last day

He was developing well, like a mushroom, in the dark.

It was an unconventional place to call a home, but he could see her like this, through the little secret crack, smell her, breathe her.

Today he was especially hungry for girl-meat.

Her hands, *if they may be called hands*, were roughly combing the orange woollen hair of her ragdoll and admonishing it for some invented misdemeanour.

"Naughty little girl childs must be punished for their sins." She was saying.

Saliva trickled its way down the overgrown forest of hairs on his chin. He would soon enough teach her something about punishment. He would soon enough show her something about sin.

He lurched and was ready to spring. The sound of something stopped him. Footsteps. They were outside her room, footsteps getting closer, quiet footsteps, clandestine, footsteps which didn't want to announce their presence.

Her hung clothes moved around him in the closet like the gentle waters of a stream. He receded with them, disappeared into his darkness.

Who is it who this way comes?

He would wait and see.

Avery's Room, the last day

"You're a naughty little girl child. A very naughty little girl child."

She was jabbering away at her ragdoll when Gabriel crept into her room. The windows were wide open, and the cool spring breeze had found its way inside, making the pink check curtains billow out like the voluminous skirts of latter-day dancing maids.

His father was out, '*Have to work this Saturday*', he'd told them. That was either true or a lie to escape the awkwardness between them. There was no time to call him. No time to call the police.

He'd just been in his parents' room and tried to get the gun they had they farmer's licence for out from the small case. But the password wasn't working. GABRIEL or GABRIEL MARK was what they used for everything. Had his father changed it last night after he'd punched him in the face, was he feeling so much contempt for him now that he couldn't even bare the mention of his name?

Either way, Gabriel would have to face whatever he had to face naked and unarmed, his sister was in there. His sister was in trouble. His sister needed him.

"Naughty little girl childs must be punished for their sins." She cautioned her doll. Then looked up to see him standing there, pent up with stress and anxiety. "What's wrong?" she chirpily said.

Gabriel nodded, and held up a finger, bidding her to be quiet, as he crossed the carpet towards her bed.

The soft pinkness of the room, so pleasant to relax in at any other time, was now draining like his blood, to weak listless shades of grey. Turning, in his imagination, to the hell he was certain the room now contained. Cushions were stones, bed covers dark, and urine stained, her stuffed toys were animals in a woodland at night,

128

their button eyes staring wildly at him, knowing he was meat for the beast. Knowing he was walking prey. He forced himself the few steps on towards her, begging himself not to feint.

He glanced at the wardrobe to his left and his flesh began to curdle on his bones. The doors were open a crack, and within the strip of darkness a sliver of a rough and sketchy half-crazed faced, the single eye he could see, glittering as it stared at him was piggish and frightful. His hearted chugged unevenly, like a heart about to stall.

He slowly sat on the edge of her bed. "Avery," he said in a voice that didn't seem real. "Avery come here."

"What's wrong?" she said again and grinned at his strange behaviour.

"Come here." He said authoritatively.

She clambered up and trotted over. He immediately gathered her in as if hugging her and pressed his mouth to her ear. "Go down the stairs, go out the front door, knock at all the neighbours' houses till you find someone home. Tell them to call the police."

When he let her go and she drew back her face was pale and frightened. "Wha-" she started to say.

He quickly put his finger to her lips to silence her.

She pulled it away and whispered. "What about you?"

"I'll be five minutes behind you."

He pushed her towards the door. She hovered there, looking fearfully back at him.

I'd rather die beside you than be in this world without you.

He nodded at her sternly. He heard her crying as she disappeared, her footsteps like little thunderclaps as they hurried down the stairs.

When he heard the front door open, he got slowly up.

Legs, please, don't fail me.

Walking back through the room was like swimming through cement.

He glanced in the triple mirrors that sat on her dresser in time to see the reflection of the wardrobe doors opening behind him and the four fingers of a man's hand curling round their edge like the legs of a spider.

That was all he needed to break though the terror that gripped him and flee.

Martin Black Senior, the last day

He'd nearly had it! Devilish bitch!

Why did he wait?

He could have had her.

He'd come as close as he had a week earlier when he smashed his way into their car. The same young man had protected her then, breaking his nose in the process. Now here he was protecting her again, this time getting her out of the house and out of his reach.

He had forgiven him for the broken nose. He wouldn't forgive him this.

He did owe the boy a great debt. Breaking into the attic through the roof was easy. He had enough food and water to last a week, he thought he'd have to wait it out there, watch her as and when he could, through the tiniest slats in the ceiling, smash his way through and into the house the first time they left her alone there.

But when the boy and his friend opened the door for him one week ago, he was able to follow them down via the ladder and enjoy a week in the quiet corners and hidden crevices of their sleek modern mansion.

The utility room in the basement was roomiest, and where he'd spent many nights.

The airing cupboard warmest, and gave him the most thrill, whenever mum of the house came along, he could never be sure whether she might open the door and find him there. He'd have given her a big 'boo!' and then unfortunately have had to strangle her with one of her newly washed sheets.

But the closet, the closet was best. He knew she'd seen him once or twice. The door was open a crack, just a crack. She'd glanced in and seen it, a green disembodied eye staring out at her.

Luckily, he had time to slip into her bathroom when she went scampering off like the little possum to bring big brother back to investigate.

Why did he wait? He cursed himself again, as he lurched from the closet and went after the boy.

He knew why. He waited because he was the cat and she was the mouse, and like any sly feline, he had roguish and rascally games to play. He liked her fear the best, the smell of it. He liked creeping out of the closet to watch her at night. He'd thought of a pillow over her face, but only if she woke up first and saw him standing there. It was important she know it was him snuffing out her life.

But even the smothering caress of a pillow was too gentle.

He wanted them all out of the house so he could have his fun with her, tear himself off strips of girl-mate. Feast on her raw flesh right in front of as she howled and begged and screamed.

Someone was going to pay, here, today, one way or another he'd have the vengeance for which he came.

He was on the boy by the time he'd gotten halfway down the stairs. He reached over the balustrade and grabbed at his head. The boy screamed and tore himself away, leaving a handful of mahogany brown hair in his balled fist.

He surprised himself for how spritely he was. At his age, and despite having spent a week crouched in cramped spaces, the bloodlust in his bones was making an Olympian out of him.

He charged at the boy in the living room, leaping on him and they both crashed heavily onto the couch. The boy on his back, he on top, his hands clamping with iron hard strength round his throat as he began to throttle the life out of him.

Oh god.

No.

This wasn't right.

The boy had done nothing. He didn't deserve this as fate. He was a boy of gentle manners and good character, of sweetness and innocence. A boy the likes of which any father would be proud of. Like Martin, *his Martin.*

God, forgive me.

He could never subject another father to feel what he'd had to feel.

He could strangle the life out of the boy here and now. Snap his neck with his big powerful hands. But his death would make another man a monster. A father ruined by grief. A father left with a mind that could not think, a heart that could not beat, a soul that could need reason. Someone else would be falling deeper and deeper into the darkness that he now only knew. His nightmare world where horror spawned horror and at dusk the devil came.

"It's ok, you're ok," he told the boy as his hands released from his neck and went to the sides of his face, soothing, comforting him. "It's ok, daddy's here."

He bent forward to kiss him gently, saliva drooling from his mouth and dripping into the boy's face.

The boy coughed and reeled and fought for his life. Suddenly a crack, as shocking and unexpected as the crack to the nose a week earlier when he'd fought to get hold of it in the car. This time to the side of his head.

Young man how many times are we doing to have to play this game?

Gabriel had reached the vase from the coffee table and smashed it around his head.

With the shock of it, Martin Black Senior reeled back, giving Gabriel opportunity to escape. Black grabbed the back of his shirt, suddenly enraged again. Gabriel darted off like a runner at a starter pistol, tearing himself out of his shirt and leaving it in Black's hands. The speed of his escape, the adrenaline and fear, the tangle of limbs and the chaos of the moment was enough to discombobulate Gabriel. He fell forcefully, awkwardly, right through the centre of the glass coffee table which smashed to a dozen butcher knife pieces underneath, one of which went through his kneecap, severing the tendons which held it in place.

Avery, the last day

She was standing in the street doing a little dance of terror and whining thinly in the Spring breeze.

None of the neighbours were home. None were answering at least.

She'd gotten halfway down the road then turned back, looking for Gabriel. He'd said he would only be five minutes behind her, but she was sure it was longer than that by now.

A week ago she'd been brotherless, alone in the world, other than a mother that didn't like her very much and whichever man she'd taken up with that week.

Now she had a heart that had found a way to beat. A heart that on one side had his name and on the other side the word . . . *'everything'.* She realised that her life before him had only been an existence. Losing him now would be like losing her arms. She could not lose him. She would not lose him. She had no idea how to say goodbye to her 'everything.'

Like someone terrified of drowning nearing the edge of a lake, she nervously took baby steps back to the kitchen window.

Gabriel was in there, on his backside, edging his way backwards across the marble tiles, leaving a blood trail behind him from under his right leg.

Then she saw him. He was looming in the kitchen doorway, bearing down on her brother, her Gabriel, his eyes alive with hate and madness.

"Gabriel," she breathed.

She'd tried so hard with his stupid son. She'd tried to get everything right, show him what an angel she could be. She'd tried to make him love her. It wasn't her fault that the men in that family were a couple of raving dribbling man-beasts.

She thought of going back in, grabbing that stupid hundred-pound chef's knife the old cow loved so much, give him a little taste of what his son gave her mother. But fate came to their aide. The old fool slipped and skidded in the blood Gabriel was leaving on the tiles and skated about like a drunk ice dancer before crashing heavily to his knees.

Ha!

Amid the insanity she felt like laughing.

Gabriel had pulled himself up and was hobbling through the door.

"Gabriel!" she screamed and ran towards him.

"Run!" he ordered. "Don't wait for me."

But she would not leave her darling brother. She positioned herself under him like a crutch and together they made it out of the drive and a short way down the street before he was nearly on them again.

"Why did you do it!" he bellowed as he chased after them.

They turned to face him, inching backwards.

"It's ok," Black said softly to Gabriel. "I just want to talk to her, ok?"

He took a swipe in her direction.

"Get away from her!" Gabriel yelled, forcing her protectively behind him.

"Stuff it up your bollocks man-pig!" Avery twisted out from Gabriel's side to scream.

His face collapsed again in thunder, the sight of her making any façade of humanity slip away and the scrawled lines of hell appear like a mask on his face. "Why did you do it?" he demanded again and made a sudden bolt.

Fate.

Again, it played its part.

Perhaps God had chosen to watch them closely that day.

The three-axel articulated lorry careered towards him. The rubber burning screech of impossibly large tyres, a frantic horn, the gasps of passers-by, rushing towards them, no time to stop, the lorry slammed into Black, obliterating him from their sight like a paper doll blown away by a breeze.

Avery screamed.

Gabriel grabbed her and pulled her into him, burying her face in his chest.

The truck driver stumbled from his cab, made it to the other side of the lorry where he vomited violently.

Gabriel put Avery into the arms of a woman who'd come to help and hobbled to the other side of the truck where the driver was still retching.

The road was now decorated with gargantuan bright red splashes of blood as though someone had dropped a giant can of paint.

Laying to the side of the curb was one of Martin Black senior's arms, severed at the elbow.

Gabriel, hobbled further round to see Martin's disembodied jawbone lying by the truck's wheels. Fighting the urge to pass out or join the driver in a copious bout of vomiting, he used the side of the truck for support and slowly made his way to its back and found what was left of Martin; his legs twisted at sickeningly strange angles, his ruined, smashed-in, jawless face, staring with wild still living eyes.

He held his one remaining hand out to Gabriel and pointed a last desperate finger in Avery's direction.

Gabriel closed his eyes.

By the time he opened them again to take another look at Martin Black senior he had succumbed to the welcomed and necessary enveloping blanket of death and was on his way to see his son again, in whatever place men who've lived such lives and carried out such acts, end up on the other side of their bonds of earthly existence.

Detective McNally, the last day

Detective McNally paced the room in front of Oliver and Vivien.

"I don't understand I thought he'd been sectioned." Said Vivien

"Yes, so did I, unfortunately." McNally said and laid a set of pictures out on his desk in front of them. They were police crime scene pictures of their own home, a small area of their loft, decked out with an old rug, a tatty pillow, the remains of food and water. Similar set ups in other lesser frequented spots in their munificent house. "As far as we can tell he'd been there almost as long as she has."

"Did he hurt her?" Oliver asked, "Did he touch her? Did he?" he added urgently.

"She told us the same thing she told to you." Said McNally. "A strange man coming into her room at night. But other than that, I think this is the first physical contact there's really been."

"Was he a psychopath?" asked Vivien.

"He was a monster." Oliver replied without looking her way.

McNally leant on the desk in front of them. "He invaded your home Mr Carsten, and your family, to you that makes him something animal and ugly. But I think he's just a father who's lost his son - his whole family. He was looking for answers in a world that had no answers to give him. Grief can make you do fucked up things."

Oliver and Vivien glanced instinctively at each other, then looked away.

"How's Gabriel?" the detective asked.

Oliver shifted awkwardly in his seat. "He's severed the tendons in his right knee. He won't be able to walk on it for a while. But they're letting me take him home in an hour. He'll have to have surgery next week."

"Brave boy." Said McNally. "You must be very proud of him."

Oliver gave him a small smile.

A phone rang on the other side of McNally's office.

He nodded that he would be just a second and headed away to answer, leaving Oliver and Vivien in a miasma of stiff tension.

Vivien got up, opened McNally's door and was about to leave. She turned back and looked down at her husband.

"You be sure and watch over our son Oliver Carsten." She said.

He played with his hands in his lap, refusing to look at her.

She regarded him an icy moment, took off her wedding ring and tossed it down on the desk next to the pictures of the crime scenes.

When McNally came back from his telephone call he found them both gone.

Chapter Ten

Tia, the last night

Vivien sat on the floor in Tia's living room in front of a small glowing fire.

She opened her laptop and accessed the picture of Oliver with the woman in the park.

Tia looked over the top of a magazine, saw what she was doing. "Stop torturing yourself."

Vivien ignored her and continued staring obsessively at the picture.

"Forgive me." Tia said sarcastically. "Forgot you always have to be torturing someone."

Tia flicked to the next page of the magazine and did a strange double take.

Just as Vivien was taking her advice and closing the lid of the laptop Tia suddenly called out. "Stop!" She got urgently off the couch and stared at the picture of Oliver with the woman in the park. "Does anyone in your house subscribe to the Insider?"

Vivien shrugged, perplexed.

Tia turned round the magazine to show Vivien the exact same image of the woman in the park, only in this version she was set in an advert, next to a dark-haired model.

Tia and Vivien hunched together over the main computer, accessing the central closed circuit security footage from the Carsten's home.

"Are you sure we can access this?" Vivien asked.

"Yes, I'm sure." Said Tia "Your security company keep your past three weeks of footage on an off-site drive - you can access via a password. Do you know what it is?"

"Try 'Gabriel-Mark'."

Tia typed the name into the password box and the footage began to play.

"Oliver hasn't butchered that one yet at least." Vivien said morosely.

Tia scrolled through fuzzy black and white footage until she came to a shot of Avery accessing their laptop computer.

"Oh, here she is." Said Tia with a sense of victory.

They watched her manipulate the image of Oliver and the woman and load it onto an email.

"Clever little witch." Vivien breathed.

"She's good." Agreed Tia. "She should come and work for me."

For the first time in twenty-four hours Vivien laughed and elbowed her faithful friend in the ribs.

"Can you burn me a DVD of this?"

Tia smiled and bent down to retrieve a disk. Something stopped her in her tracks, something else she was seeing on the screen.

The smile fell instantly from her.

Vivien frowned, concerned. "What?"

Tia looked up at her friend, her eyes set with sudden anger.

"I always wondered why you never pleaded innocence." Tia said. "Do you know what I thought? I thought you were protecting Gabriel. Thought maybe he was unwell somehow and he was the

142

one to blame, putting something in her drinks. In the back of my mind, I knew you'd never harm a child."

Tia stepped aside and revealed footage of Avery dropping household cleaning products and bleach into her own orange juice. "How long were you going to punish Oliver before you let him know the truth?" Tia asked.

After a long awkward moment Vivien answered. "Until I brought him to his knees."

Tia let out a small incredulous laugh.

"You're so determined Vivien." She said. "And so strong. But my god you're cautious. And you're so . . . unforgiving. Of even the most basic vagaries of the human heart."

The trace of a tear came to Vivien's eye, but her face remained stony.

"All the time I've known you we've discussed Oliver and his weaknesses, his little slips, and what they mean." Said Tia. "But my girl you've beat the best of them this time. And your stubborn heart means you've left your only child under a roof with a clever little angel who isn't only excellent at manipulating computer images and emails . . . she's also rather good at manipulating human beings."

Avery, the last night, 7.20 p.m.

What does it take for a little heart to finally be complete?

A father, giving you the key to the house so you can open the door for him. It's stiff and tough to turn, cold metal digging in tiny fingertips. But that doesn't matter, that doesn't matter at all. You've an important job to do, you must get the door open because dad's coming home with Gabriel in his arms. Carrying him in like a Christmas tree.

Christmas will be just as exciting and magical as this day when it comes around in another nine months' time.

They'd get the biggest tree in the lot. Dad would shake his head, but she and Gabriel would insist, and he'd laugh and give way to their demands, they'd have three big hot chocolates in the café within the Christmas Tree shop and then they'd carry it to the car together. Dad and Gabe taking the heavy end, her holding the tip. She would have an important job too. Just as important as getting the door open now so dad could carry Gabriel in.

She tripped ahead of them, dizzy with excitement, pushing chairs and plants out of the way. Dad needed a clear path to carry Gabriel through. It was her job to make sure he had that clear path. It would always be her job to make sure dad had a clear path, it would always be her job to get the front door open, it would always be her job to carry the tip of the Christmas tree.

"Ouch," Gabriel muttered.

Oh no.

She hadn't pushed the tall light stand far enough to the right and dad had knocked his leg against it as he'd brought him through the hall.

144

Oh no. Oh no. Poor Gabe.

They saw the distress on her face, and both laughed. Not at her, of course. But because she was so adorable. She loved and worried so about her brother.

Had there ever been a time for any of them where they hadn't been together, like this?

She couldn't remember such a time and she was certain that neither could they. This was a moment cut right out of time just for her, like a slice from a great big cake. She would steal it into her heart and lock it away there forever.

And later that night another slice of memory to be carved out of the cake of time for her, an even better one.

"Avery, I need you to look after your brother for a while. I've got to go into the office to get some papers." Said Oliver.

Oh daddy, daddy, of course I will. I'll read to him and comb his hair and I'll get him pills if his leg hurts too much and if he falls asleep, I'll sit and watch him till you get home and everything will be ok.

I love you daddy.

I love you Gabe.

Gabriel, the last night, 7.47 p.m.

"Are you comfortable?" Oliver asked.

Gabriel nodded. He wasn't. His leg was throbbing as though someone had just hacked it off below the knee with a rusty blade. But he knew he wasn't always the son his father wanted; the agreeing nod hopefully would be enough for him to be 'tough' in front of him, 'a man'.

Oliver fished into the paper bag for the pain relief pills they'd been sent home from the hospital with. He popped one out through the silver encasement and handed it to Gabriel, with an *'I know you better than you think'* smile.

"Take another two of these in a couple of hours." Oliver said. "They'll knock you right out. I'll carry you up to your room when I get in."

Oliver plumped a cushion and eased it behind Gabriel's back on the couch, tidied the hair out of his eyes. For a moment they stared at each other, as if taking in their respective hearts.

"Dad," Said Gabriel. "Is it alright if I have someone over tonight?" Adding quickly. "Don't worry, it's just Lisa. It's not Reece."

Oliver smiled warmly at his son and something within that smile said, *'Why didn't I ever notice when you became a man?'*

"Of course you can." He said. "You can have over whoever you want."

Oliver ruffled the hair he'd tidied minutes earlier, got up and went to the door. He stopped, as if he'd forgotten his keys, came back to the couch and kissed the top of his son's head.

Gabriel smiled and watched him leave.

146

I love you, I love you, I love you.

So thumped the beat of his heart.

Vivien, 7.47 p.m. the last night

Vivien, threw her bag in the back of her car and frantically opened the driver's side door, hurrying to get inside, until something about the world around her slowed her to a deathly pace.

The apple trees were yet to bud, two weeks late nearly, a by-product of global warming, another sign of man's rape and destruction of the earth he was given. Instead of bursting with the promise of Spring they looked felled and dead. Their shadows lengthened and they had all but eaten the sun.

The sky above was an aching nothing. Great clouds shifted like slowly moving continents letting scars of indigo light appear and vanish, appear and vanish.

It was a night full of sibilant whispers.

It was a night hushed, as if remembering.

It was a night that held its breath, as if waiting for the word of the wind.

It was a night with a message for Vivien Carsten:

Dear lady, don't you know? When a lamb is lost on a mountain side, they will cry like a baby in a crib. When the mother lamb hears she comes running. However, there are times the wolf also hears. The mother's love is stronger, but the wolf's legs are faster. And that is the way of things.

And when the wind did come its voice was malignant, its words were shrill. And the words on its breath were '*murder, murder, murder.*'

Vivien got into her car and tore out of Tia's drive and down the adjoining road, its engine revving like a dying scream.

Avery, 8.24 p.m. the last night

It was a work of art.

She gazed down at the tray, prouder of it than she had ever been of any of her sketches. Or any of the images she'd cobbled together with her advanced photoshopping skills.

The sandwich was cheese and pickle, his favourite. The crips, ready salted - the flavour must come from the sandwich you see. The drink; a coke with six lumps of ice. Gabriel likes his drinks so cold they make your mouth go all numby. A piece of squidgy chocolate fudge cake for afters. But wait – a napkin folded into the shape of a swan. Ta-dah! It had taken her nearly an hour to do it. She'd had a YouTube video on and followed it step by step. He'd be so amazed he never would believe she'd taught herself how to do it just that night. And just for jolly, a little snapshot of the two of them. She'd had to photoshop it and print it on daddy's printer. There wasn't a real picture of the two of them together just yet. But that was ok, soon enough there would be.

A work of art.

A thing of beauty.

She sighed as she looked at it. She couldn't wait to see his face.

She carried it as carefully as a high wire trapeze artist, face set in heavy concentration.

One step, two step,

Careful, mustn't spill a drop of coke.

Three step, four step

He'll call me 'his little chef'.

Five step, six step,

I found you, I found you, I found you.

So thumped the beat of her-

She reached him.

She slammed the tray down on the coffee table. Coke flew in the air and cascaded down, dousing the napkin swan, and making her head sink to one side as if someone had snapped her long graceful neck.

She took an angry step towards him. "Who's she?!!"

Gabriel, 8.25 p.m. the last night

"What do you think you're doing? Get out of here. I'm on a date." Barked Gabriel.

Beside him Lisa was scrabbling to pull her sweater back on over her bare breasts.

"Didn't dad tell you?" he asked his scowling little half-sister.

"No." she fired at him like a disgruntled thirty-year-old. "He didn't."

Avery, 8.35 p.m. the last night

She had the lid of her felt tip pen in her mouth like the stub of a cigar and was sketching in her pad furiously. So fervent and enraged were her pen strokes she looked like an old master at work, as if possessed by the hand of God.

She was sitting at the top of the landing above them, tiny legs poking through the gaps in the balustrade's railing and swinging wildly. Surprisingly strong legs for such a slight little eleven-year-old.

So, the top's back off now is it you dirty little bitch face?

I've got bigger tits than you and I'm not even seventeen.

Slag bag doxie tramp.

What the f-

Avery stopped her artwork to study Gabriel and the girl with him more closely. She was bending down near his thingy.

Oh my god! Was she trying to eat it?

Should she call the police? Was she a vampire? Was she trying to bite it off of him. What the hell was wrong with that lickspittle harpy?

She thought of going down and grabbing the tray she'd left discarded on the coffee table. Whacking it unceremoniously over the back of that smellfungus wench's head. Gabriel would thank her and scoop her into his arms and kiss her and-

Oh my gosh!

It was something he was enjoying! Telling her not to stop, not shrieking at her to get off of him. He was even holding the back

of her head and pushing her down in all the right places, moaning and yap-yap-yapping like a drunk old chimpanzee.

She wondered if daddy knew what a dirty little snollygoster his milksop of mama's boy really was.

She made sure she got the big greasy smile on his face in the picture she was drawing. His big greasy smile and all the nasty penis eating.

That and all the other arse salad that was going on down there too.

She would make sure she captured every one of the sick sick sicko dirty dirty things.

Vivien, 9.12 p.m. the last night

She tapped the touch screen on the car's panel and tried Oliver's number for the seventh time.

She stared fixedly at the road ahead of her. A cold dew covered her forehead, her scalp itched, her limbs her numb. She was yellow and sick. Yellow from glare of the unforgiving streetlamps forcing its way through her windows.

Sick with the infection of fear.

The call to Oliver went unanswered again.

"Dammit Oliver." She hissed to herself and tapped her son's name on the screen.

Gabriel, 9.13 p.m. the last night

As he closed the door on Lisa he heard is phone ringing upstairs.

"Avery get my phone!" he called.

Nothing came back to him from the upper floor but silence.

"Avery!"

He used the wall and side tables for support to hobble to the foot of the stairs.

He could hear the persistent ringing of his phone coming from the bathroom.

What was she doing in there with it?

"Avery!"

Avery, 9.25 p.m. the last night

What was to be done about Gabriel Mark Carsten?

What was to be done about Gabe?

What indeed?

Avery Miller laid in the £2,503.50 Kohler Stargaze freestanding bath and mused over just what should be done about the disappoint and betrayal her half-brother had just beset upon her. Her long hair floated out behind her like an oil slick spreading on a tide, and the hot steamy water filled her ears, helping to drown out the sound of the pansy little milksop mama's boy who was still bleating on and on about his phone from downstairs.

As if on cue his phone rang again and the face of the old crone lit up on the small screen. She'd called about a thousand times. *Christ, could she take a hint that no one wanted to talk to her?*

And what was the deal with that picture? Botoxed up to the eyeballs in life and filtered within an inch of it virtually. *Give up the ghost sister, go gracefully to the grave, you've had your day.*

Avery splashed about like a kipper and her bare wet knees hit the side of the bath. The phone wobbled precariously, like a great building about to topple after an earthquake. Then fell forward, Vivien's grinning picture still set in the screen, and landed SPLOSH! right in the middle of her bathwater where it hissed and fizzed and drown drown drowned down below her feet. *Oops! Accidents will happen. Yes they will.*

What was to be done about Gabriel Mark Carsten?

156

What was to be done about Gabe?

What indeed?

It wasn't the only thought that was catapulting around in her brain. In truth there were a thousand of them, screaming in every direction like a hysterical crowd fleeing a blaze.

Thoughts were tiring. She wanted to be free of them. But in all the short years of her life she'd never managed to escape the crazy dancers that twirled and twisted and kicked up their feet, feet that banged inside her, flying fists that punched in her skull, a bellowing throng that screamed her name. All she wanted was her own cup of stars. Was that so terrible? Something warm to wrap her up in. Bring her light on the darkest of nights. Keep her toasty on the coldest of days.

She'd tried so often, with every lunchbox boring, man of the week, her poor dead mother had shacked up with. But in the end, they all let her down. They all had to be dealt with.

And now, so did Gabe.

She got out of the bath, slippery and wet, and made her way towards his camera. She'd left it on the back of the £1,578 Kohler wall hung toilet, its setting still ready to take selfies from a distance. He'd showed her how earlier that week and promised they get one of them together some day.

He'd betrayed her. Humiliated her. And that had left nothing but scar tissue on her heart. Dead and decaying cells in her brain. He only had himself to blame.

You take everything from me, take, take, take.

The most wicked thing in the world, she thought, was the inability of those we love to feel the wrongs they inflict upon us. We live on an island of hope and ruin and the war dead lie littered in the streets. We shall all either go mad from the want and longing of a better tomorrow and die and join them. Or stand and fight and

157

make those who crushed us into great balls of sorrow understand the hell they've made.

Avery Miller crossed the bathroom with her wet sopping feet towards Gabriel's camera, her little mind burning alive with the fire of intent.

Your smile once cauterised my wounds.

Your love once brought me into aliveness.

Now you carve me up with your cruelty and leave my soul to bleed.

There was not time for childhood's dark games and imaginings.

She was a child no longer.

Oliver, 10.01 p.m. the last night

Oliver sat on the side of the couch where Gabriel slept and wished he could have taken back time. The last three days would do it. The thought of hitting him the second time was like a cut that never heals.

He would apologise to him in the morning.

He had planned to do so tonight on his way home from the office. Vivien had called consistently. Consistently he'd ignored her. With all the trouble and trauma they'd endured that week he couldn't say he was happy. But for the first time in seven days he felt pleased.

Earlier that evening he'd felt a reconnection with the son he'd loved all his life and a bond with the daughter he still barely knew. It was as though the heavy acrid dust of disruption had settled and cleared the air for what was meant to be.

And that was the last moment of Oliver Carsten's life, before lightening split his world and everything changed forever.

Gabriel's camera blinked at him from the coffee table. His son had obviously been scrolling through the photo-gallery, before succumbing to the drug heavy sleep no doubt. But the little screen of ghostly white was a door to the dead. Oliver knew it. He could make out the image. A girl's naked form standing with her back to the camera, slippery and wet. A girl years, *years*, under the age of eighteen.

This cannot be my life.

This ghost of a life.

My son cannot be a monster.

Oliver Carsten closed his eyes and met the face of his dead brother. He hadn't even had the courtesy to wait for him in his dreams.

Tad smiled a broad lipless smile to Oliver, his black tongue poking out through puffy gums and broken teeth. *'It's a family thing Oliver old boy.'* He hissed. *'A family thing. Told you he was part of me.'*

Oliver's eyes flew open, shutting Tad out as though turning off a television screen.

He stood urgently up. Gabriel stirred but didn't awaken.

He grabbed the camera and clicked through the pictures. The girl with her back to the camera slowly turned round in the succession of pictures and the truth came off his flesh like a scent. For a moment, as she turned with stop-motion stiltedness, he was certain he would see Ellie's face, dead eyes still ringed with black mascara, the same haunted look in them that begged for him to save her.

But the eyes that begged and the skin that was revealed, the little barely formed breasts that were put on show, the tiny buttocks that were posed and the pretty young pussy that was made to spread and become a pervert's evil art, were not his sister's.

They were his daughter's.

His Avery.

Avery, 10.20 p.m. the last night.

The pink room breathed at him, but there was no other sound.

He had been sitting on the edge of his daughter's bed watching her sleep since he'd come upstairs with the camera and found the second catalogue of evidence in her sketchpad, crude rudimentary drawings, in bright waxy colours, which told a dark and depraved tale.

He wished they could stay this way for every. The two of them, statues, frozen in a moment of time. When she woke, when she opened her eyes, he would have to speak of it. He would have to open his own eyes. He would be condemned to the things he had no wish to know, forever haunted by the words he didn't want to hear or say.

His great chest moved up and down like the swell of an ocean, moving with the Spring wind that found its way in through the window and skated over her pale listless face.

Before she opened her eyes, she knew he was watching. Felt the weight of his gaze just as much as the soft wind on her cheeks.

"Hi daddy," she said groggily.

He had her sketchpad in his lap and Gabriel's camera on her little bedside table.

"Avery," he said quietly. And his voice sounded like that of a stranger.

She wriggled up in bed to look solemnly at him.

"Avery," he said again. "Is this the man who comes in your room to look at you at night?"

He nodded down to the sketchbook, to the picture she'd made of that milksop mama's boy and the chewy on the pee pee thing that wretched unsufferable slag-hag was doing to him.

She cast her eyes sadly to her lap.

"Avery," he said sternly, drawing them back to him. "How often has he been in your room?"

She let the ensuing silence stretch. Seeping through the room and around them like a tide. Finally, she glanced at the camera on the bedside table next to her, watching her like an unblinking eye. She looked back at her father and answered him. "Every day."

The Grand PooBah of all Monstrous Fuck Ups, the last night

Gabriel woke with a violence in his face that needed to be earned somehow. His cheek shattering with the aggression of a bomb, bursting with the force of an exploding sun.

This would have to be a dream.

He closed his eyes to be able to open them again to the reassuring stillness of the home he knew.

Instead, he opened them to a hell he could only guess at as being something that was really happening.

The man who should have loved him most, protected him beyond anything, sat on the couch beside him, with a gun in his hand. The gun he'd just used to awaken his son from his dreams by smashing it into his face and fracturing his cheek.

Gabriel put a hand up to catch the line of blood. He was blinded suddenly in his right eye and thought his entire eyeball may fall out any second, hang on its stalk like some obscene monstrous thing. But it was only the effluence of blood, marring his vision.

He did his best to blink it away and looked to his father. For a moment there was only silence, silence bar the beating of two unsure hearts.

"Why?" Gabriel said breathlessly.

His father's only answer was to point the gun his way.

A ripple of uncertainty softened his father's heart. He tossed the gun onto the coffee table, grabbed his beleaguered son's arms, and heaved him off the couch.

Gabriel crawled across the kitchen floor on his ruined knee. Putting a frail pathetic attempt up to touch his bleeding face and get away from his approaching father.

Oliver moved behind him at a slow measured pace.

He reached him and with the heartlessness of a killer trod down on his knee. Gabriel screamed and fell against the cabinets, shocked and nauseated.

Oliver picked him up and dropped him unceremoniously down on the kitchen table, reaching for the nearest weapon he could find, Vivien's £109.99 Damascus double edge chef's knife, which he held like a street robber in his son's face.

"Tell me you did it, tell me why you did it." He demanded.

"Did what? Dad!" Gabriel begged, frightful tears flooding his face.

Oliver's heart made a lurch into his throat. *What was he doing? What was he doing to his boy?* He awoke, as if from a trance.

My god, what have I done?

Gabriel remained trembling in his grip and for a moment they regarded each other, as if trying to help one another out of the insanity.

For the first time in his life Gabriel saw his father weep. Not the quiet ebbing of tears. The torrential sobbing of despair and disbelief.

They slipped from the table together, Oliver cradling his son's poor uncontrollably shaking body in his arms.

Oliver held him as if they were going down together on a sinking ship and continued to wail a desperate painful howling lament that sounded like a slowly devoured animal's dying scream.

"It's ok dad. It's ok. Please." Gabriel reached up with a trembling hand and gently touched his father's cheek.

She appeared in the kitchen in front of them, hiding her face in a creamy swing of blonde.

Oliver rocked his wounded son but soon found himself drawn back to the Ellie-Avery, sister-daughter, looking at him from the other side of the kitchen, eyes beseeching him for help. Eyes, saying, *'What about me?'*

Oliver found himself shrinking until he was in her tiny house, looking out through the window of her eyes.

She was looking at the father who had brought her unwillingly into this world. Left her to a life where men broke a thousand promises, came, and went, and did God knows what whenever they wanted. She only existed because of his selfishness, his sin. His betrayal of his wife. His indulgence. His reluctance to wear a condom. Then he'd brought her into the heart of his house and into the hands of his monstrous brother-offspring, his other Tad, who'd then, behind closed doors, done another Ellie thing.

And now here he was, betraying her as he had betrayed Ellie, leaving her to the wolves again, holding her Tad-monster to his heart, covering up his sin with lies, painting her defilement up into something so forgivable, so pretty.

'I love you Ellie-Avery,' he said with his eyes. *'And I'm so so sorry.'* And it was their moment. A moment just for the two of them.

He loved her so much he could drown in her.

And she knew it.

And so, her eyes looked back and said *'I love you too. But now it's time daddy . . . kill'.*

The high end £109.99 Damascus Chef's Kitchen knife with a double-edged blade in his hand tore through the Tad-Gabriel thing's skin and sinew and ripped and savaged and gashed it apart. It made short work of his superior laryngeal artery. Sliced and severed his jugular vein. Punctured his sternothyroid muscle. Destroyed the inferior root of his ansa cervicalis. Carved up his hypoglossal nerve.

Gabriel let out nothing but a low moaning cry in his final death-agonies.

Oliver looked down to the corpse in his arms, to the terrors he'd created, to the death of his first-born child, his only son, fitting with the last frail fragments of life. His death, at his hands.

He looked over to her, as if for explanation, or support.

Then saw what else he had created.

She peered out from between the curtains of blonde, and on her face was a smile, a smile that said *death, death, death, I win, I win, I win.*

Her eyes widened and he could see the intention in her face, the murderous gleam.

He looked down at his son's slain body.

His innocent son, his child, who only loved and never harmed and throughout his life bore the brunt of his father's rages and moods and slips. And now bore the fatal wounds of what could be truly crowned his monumental fuck up. The colossal king of all fuck ups, the bastard son of the Grand Poobah of mother fucking monstrous wrongness of wrongs.

The fucking end of everything.

"Oh my god, my son, Gabriel, Gabriel!" he screamed.

And the nightmare unlidded like a dark deep eye. A nightmare black enough to kick and bite. A nightmare that tore through a £100,000 designer kitchen like a hurricane and with equally destructive ferocity picked up everything in its path and tore it to a thousand pieces.

The Hour of the Great Mistake, the last night

Vivien Carsten arrived home beneath a terrible sky.

A night sky turning maroon, like the colour of dried blood.

She had given up her frantic efforts to reach either her husband or her son and instead tried Detective John McNally.

"Do you know what time it is? What's wrong? Why do you want me to meet you at your house?"

"Please!!!" she had screamed.

Whether he had taken her seriously or not she did not know. Whether he was coming or not she did not know.

If he was coming, she had beaten him there.

As she came into the living room, the stillness of the house brought great comfort and helped convince her her concerns were nothing but imagination.

Until she saw the gun, lying on the coffee table, ringed by a splatter of blood that gleamed in the moonlight.

She kept it in her hand until she reached the kitchen.

A glutinous darkness swamped the room from either side. A little further back, the shape of the island could be discerned. Other shapes descended until they were lost in shadows. She came forward. Those shapes where what she had come here to see.

The horror of it threatened to break every bone in her body in one hideous crack. The hell of it seemed almost sweet and morphic, preordained, the only righteous punishment for her and her great mistake. Oliver wasn't exempt from the most monstrous of fuck ups, she'd just joined him in one from which there would be no escape. She'd left her child in this house, with the devil itself.

That storm would rage in her heart forever, trash it until there was nothing left of it but stone and wood, kept alive by a few shards of tissue and ruined vessels and nerves, pumping with a frail and tragic beat.

For a moment her rage was so great she could not speak. The blood crushed so loudly in her ears she could not hear. The cold horror squeezing her throat so colossal it left her unable to breathe.

Finally, her voice came to her and set off like a fire whistle gone insane as screamed her dead son's name.

She used all her failing strength to force the gun in her hand under her husband's chin. He was sitting numbly on the kitchen floor holding their dead child limply in his arms, surrounded by the gore and blood of his murder.

Oliver looked blankly at her, the tiny flicker of life in his eyes seemed to say *'please, pull that trigger, send me to hell, quickly.'*

The torture of it was not enough to make a murderer of her. She dropped the gun before she changed her mind and used it on Oliver and fell to the floor and cradled her slain child and howled and screamed.

The gunshot rang out above her, bursting her eardrum and leaving her with permanent tinnitus and other irreparable damage. Oliver was dead before he hit the granite tiles, the bullet from the gun in his own hand having ripped through his brain.

As she turned away, she saw it.

It was sitting in the corner of the kitchen like it wanted a ring side seat.

The blue flashing lights of the approaching police cars lit up through the windows like Christmas decorations and threw great moving shapes at Vivien as she lunged for it like a feral beast.

Avery knew to wait till the police were just about to enter the kitchen.

The old crone had grabbed the gun and was waving it her way. She smashed herself between the fridge and cabinet next to it and cowered and shook and squealed. "No! Don't hurt me! Please! Don't kill me!"

Detective John McNally pushed his way through the two uniformed officers to find Vivien, weapon aimed at her stepdaughter, the remnants of her son and husband lying beside her in gory bloody heaps.

The officers brought her down quickly, knocked the gun away, forced her bellicosely on to the kitchen table where she writhed and shrieked.

McNally snatched the little girl up. She buried her face in his big chest. He wrapped protective arms around her and looked back at Vivien. "What have you done? What have you done to you family?"

Chapter Eleven

Vivien, tomorrow

She was barely aware of the world around her.

She didn't know the last time she'd washed, combed her hair, changed her knickers. She knew she probably smelt. She didn't care. She wasn't sure if the prison guards treated her with contempt due to the recent indifference to her personal hygiene or their disdain for a mother who would commit that most ungodly of sins. That was the reason she was cut off from the other prisoners, outcast like a leper. They would have dashed her head off every wall in the secure section if they'd gotten their hands on her, bashed out her brain.

Let them. It would have been a blessing, a sweet release.

She didn't know the time or the day of the week. But she knew which day it was.

It was the day they were burying her son.

She was too far gone for tears. They still hadn't come. Every time she felt the steady promise of their onset, she would ultimately convulse on her cell floor in screams. Screams that would burn in her throat like acid, tear through skin and sinew and rip and savage and gash it apart. Make short work of her superior laryngeal artery. Slice and sever her jugular vein. Puncture her sternothyroid muscle. Destroy the inferior root of her ansa cervicalis. Carve up her hypoglossal nerve. Wreck her like the handiwork of a high end £109.99 Damascus Chef's Kitchen knife with a double-edged blade.

She stared ahead through the nameless moment as they gave her only child up to a deep cold grave.

She knew she was burying her soul with him. Any soul she had left may as well have been on the moon, drowning in some alien sea. Whatever was left was going into the ground, food for worms, no use to her now. No use to anyone or anything.

The two policewomen either side of her held her as Gabriel Carsten was positioned into his final resting place.

Why were they holding her? Compassion?

Possibly.

More likely they'd been here before and knew the erratic histrionics of grief. Readying themselves for the moment she'd try to tear herself away and fling herself on either her son's or her husband's coffin.

Even murderesses felt anguish.

Even the evil felt remorse.

Even the devil felt sorrow.

So it would seem.

Her broken heart stopped beating as if it had been touched by the icy finger of death.

They'd brought it.

It was back in its ugly tatty pinafore dress and scuffed Mary-Janes. Hand in the hand of another social worker and fuck ugly sock rolled down and bunched round the ankle of that bastard little leg, still expecting everyone to buy the whole '*I'm far to meek and vulnerable to pull my sock up under my knee*' routine.

Those eyes that came to her like a trauma in her every frantic moment of fitful nauseating sleep were solemnly gazing at her

172

father's coffin, then turned to her half-brother's, now, thanks to her, planted in his unreturnable grave.

Vivien couldn't move, breathe, think. She slumped between the two policewomen like a great lump of dead meat.

Finally, it turned those vile unwarrantable eyes her way.

Then it did what would have made the innocently, unjustly accused Vivien Carsten become a murderer right in front of a hundred witnesses, in front of judge, jury and executioner, without a moment's hesitation.

It smiled.

It smiled at her.

A sweet little smile of vicious evil ugly intent. A devil's goading grin. A smile she had smiled in the Carsten kitchen nine days earlier. A smile that made a murderer of her husband and a corpse of her son. A smile that would without doubt produce the exact reaction she now wanted to see.

And with that smile the bony hand of death that had touched Vivien Carsten's heart and stilled it, now squeezed it and returned her to her diseased unwelcomed life.

She knew she was screaming but heard no sound of it. Knew the handcuffs were cutting into her wrists but sensed no pain. Knew the policewomen where roughly manhandling her, holding her back, but felt nothing.

The mourners gasped, shrieked, edged away.

Tia was crying, ashen, near feinting "Oh Vivien." She wailed.

Vivien tried to nod, let her know she knew what she was doing, the same to the policewomen. "I just want to talk to her, okay?"

The social worker pulled Avery tighter into her side, scowled at Vivien with a '*haven't you and your family put her through enough?*', look of condemnation and began to draw her away.

Vivien's fight to get at her intensified, as did the policewomen's effort to control her, hustling her backwards towards the van like a stubborn beast.

"Why did you do it?!" Vivien screamed at her, her voice rising in such sharp shrill shrieks it felt formidable enough to shatter the sky above them. "Why did you do it?!!!!!"

The social worker was drawing her away from the ugly scene, ushering her into the car and pulling her back from harm just as they were throwing Vivien Carsten into the back of a police van with nothing more to be heard from her other than her final parting words "She's evil! She's brilliant!"

Words that the wind carried Avery Miller's way.

Words that reached her.

Words that bored her.

She yawned and hoped the old bitch saw that too.

Let her have that too to chew on in her dreams.

Avery, tomorrow

What was to be done about Avery Miller-Carston?

What was to be done about Avery?

What indeed?

She found herself in a car being driven back to a town she should have been running away from.

She looked up from her lap at the man driving and his wife beside him.

She hadn't taken a lot of notice of Detective McNally the first time they met. It was the day after . . . *they* . . . stole her up from her poor mother's funeral and subjected her to what no eleven-year old's ears should have to listen to. No eleven-year-old's skin should be exposed to. No eleven-year old's eyes should ever see.

She'd overheard him telling the social worker how guilty he felt for not spotting it about them, the Carstens. That . . . *grave and hidden wrongness* . . . those other . . . *certain things.*

Maybe I'll forgive you.

Maybe I won't.

We'll see.

I was a tiny little creature that day. Already battered and broken and bruised by fate. Then nearly swallowed whole by a man-monster. Only for you to scoop me up and deliver me right into the midst of a big shiny house full of other . . . monstrous things.

McNally glanced in the rear-view mirror and saw her looking at him. He smiled. A big warm comfy smile that felt like Christmas morning.

Maybe she'd forgive him.

Maybe.

The car bumped along on its clumsy journey. Right by the spot where two weeks earlier the man-beast had jumped out from between trees to try to smash into the car and gobble her up into his big beast-belly.

That Gabriel boy had made such a thing about being the hero. *What a tool.* It wasn't as though he'd made the Kessel Run in twelve par secs. All he'd done was hold on to her skirt while they drove away. Anyone would think he'd slayed a goddam dragon or something. He was never man enough to have a handle on such things.

It was only she who knew a thing or two about courage, about resourcefulness, about boundaries, about ruin, about fear.

To look fear in the face is to know who we are. Fear defines our limitations. Horror carves and shapes the soul. Horror knows our true name and walks beside us when all others turn away.

Daddy McNally was looking more and more like a man with whom she could discuss these and other matters.

The wife . . . *on the other hand* . . . she may be a different affair.

She'd heard the two of them arguing fiercely when the social worker suggested they take her with them. She'd barely looked at her following that, as if '*seeing*' the little problem that had inconvenienced her existence, now sitting in the back seat of the family car would somehow make it all real.

Don't worry sweet cheeks, you can get back soon enough to the Golf Club and your Bridge Parties, and sucking your middle finger

176

while you pour over pictures of David Gandy in his undercrackers. It must be hard for you. I'm sure your world-weary hubby is exhausted and hasn't got the energy to mount Mrs McNally when he comes home from fighting crime all day.

Up-down, up-down, up-down.

Her little leg began to kick. They had a surprising amount of force for a such slight eleven-year-old. Such a delicate little thing.

Up-down, up-down, up-down.

Kick, kick, kick.

Oops.

That last one went right into the back of Mount McMally's car seat. She didn't like that. Turned round and looked at her like she'd opened the microwave door and discovered a hot steaming piece of freshly cooked dog shit.

Surprise.

Life isn't like a box of chocolates.

But children are. You never know what you're gonna get.

He was probably about a year or two older than that Gabriel; *their son that sat beside her.* But he was twice as cool. Better clothes, better haircut. Not quite as good looking but he had a whole lotta something else.

What was it? What's there sitting in those eyes of yours? Where'd you get all that mystery and wonder?

Ah, I see it now. You got an *'as fuck'* rough edge.

He seemed to sense her studying him, fished in the back pocket of his baggy jeans and came back with a handful of sweets. Without a word, or a smile, he held them out in front of her.

I like your small clever little hands.

She chewed on the sweet and considered him.

She'd handled the exchange with much aplomb, the classy coolness of casual indifference. She didn't gasp or smile or say thank you. He wasn't some cheugy like Gabriel. And neither was she. He'd respect her for all her quiet corners.

They'd chill later, her and the big dog. Daddy McNally would look in and check they were ok. Mount Mama could sit in her room a sulk-sulk-sulking about the price of petrol and the state of the economy post Brexit and all the muckety-muck they'd got on the carpet when they dragged her suitcase up the stairs earlier that day. He'd tweet later to his friends about his new little sister *'par excellence'*. She'd help get a picture of her and him together onto his account doing some random thing. She was good at photoshopping images. She was good at manipulating things. They'd have time enough to create future memories and take photos of adventures that were real.

Then later that night they'd crackerjack to some dope tunes and chat *this and this and fucking that* about a whole heap of things.

She would have her cup of stars too. She would be like everyone else. Little dimpled girl with a smile of melting chocolate who'd earned her joy at last. She'd waited for it oh so long.

She would have it now.

With him.

Certain cylinders fired inside her. Nerves that were near dead, cells at the end of their life cycle were coming alive with the nearness of him. As if each were finding the place from where it once came. Finding its way back home.

She hadn't expected to feel like this. Like an amputee finally given her arms again.

She hadn't planned for love.

178

Brave girl. Wise brave girl. Wise brave clever girl who knew who to turn to and who to trust and finally found what she'd looked for all these years sitting next to her with a handful of sweets.

On one side of her world his name was printed, on the other just one word which said . . . . *'everything.'*

Up-down, up-down, up-down.

Kick, kick, kick.

I found you. I found you. I found you.

So thumped the beat of her heart.

The End

Printed in Great Britain
by Amazon